Samuel French Acting Ed

The Nest

by Theresa Rebeck

FOR PRODUCTION ENQUIRIES

UNITED STATES AND CANADA
Info@SamuelFrench.com
1-866-598-8449

UNITED KINGDOM AND EUROPE
Plays@SamuelFrench.co.uk
020-7255-4302

Each title is subject to availability from Samuel French, depending
upon country of performance. Please be aware that THE NEST may
not be licensed by Samuel French in your territory. Professional and
amateur producers should contact the nearest Samuel French office or
licensing partner to verify availability.

MUSIC USE NOTE

Licensees are solely responsible for obtaining formal written permission from copyright owners to use copyrighted music in the performance of this play and are strongly cautioned to do so. If no such permission is obtained by the licensee, then the licensee must use only original music that the licensee owns and controls. Licensees are solely responsible and liable for all music clearances and shall indemnify the copyright owners of the play(s) and their licensing agent, Samuel French, against any costs, expenses, losses and liabilities arising from the use of music by licensees. Please contact the appropriate music licensing authority in your territory for the rights to any incidental music.

IMPORTANT BILLING AND CREDIT REQUIREMENTS

If you have obtained performance rights to this title, please refer to your licensing agreement for important billing and credit requirements.

THE NEST premiered at the Denver Center for the Performing Arts (produced by Denver Center Theatre Company) in Denver, Colorado on January 22, 2016. The performance was directed by Adrienne Campbell-Holt, with scenic design by Lisa Orzolek, costume design by Angela Balogh Calin, lighting design by Grant W.S. Yeager, and sound design by Craig Breitenbach. The stage manager was Lyle Raper. The cast was as follows:

NED	Kevin Bernston
IRENE	Andrea Syglowski
BARRY	Brian D. Coats
PATRICK	Brian Dykstra
MARGO	Carly Street
LILA	Laura Latreille
NICK	David Mason
SAM	Victoria Mack

CHARACTERS

NED

IRENE

BARRY

PATRICK

MARGO

LILA

NICK

SAM

ACT ONE

Scene One

(A bar. Old, wood, a beautiful mirror upsta͜ /

*(**MARGO** at the bar, drinking alone. **PATRICK** and **BARRY** at the other end, having beers.)*

*(**NED** – anguished, passionate, struggling – is at a table. He is speaking to **IRENE**. **IRENE** is eating fries and having a glass of wine. **NED** is having a beer.)*

NED. It was the yellow fever. They were, bodies were stacked up on the street, like just stacked, on top of each other, like logs.

IRENE. Oh.

NED. They didn't have enough room in the cemeteries to bury them! Or, it wasn't even that they didn't have room. I think they did have room, but so many people were dying, just dying, that no one had time to bury them. They were all dying too.

IRENE. Really?

NED. I don't know all the details. But my whole family, it's kind of amazing there are any of us left, honestly. It just like devastated, and that was why people moved north, there was no one left there, this was New Orleans –

IRENE. Uh-huh.

NED. And so they moved up to Indiana, or Illinois, the Midwest, they were like –

IRENE. Who is this again?

NED. My great-great-great grandparents. Great-great – maybe just two greats.

IRENE. And they moved –

es. Because they had like no money.

NED. And they had like no one. No – they came to America thinking it was you know the promised land and –

IRENE. They moved to New Orleans?

NED. No, America. Well, yeah, New Orleans.

IRENE. Their whole family moved there?

NED. No no – they moved to America. And then some of them moved to New Orleans.

IRENE. Some of who?

(A beat.)

NED. I just, I'm sorry. I'm trying to tell this – story –

IRENE. Oh yeah.

NED. I mean –

IRENE. No no no sorry.

NED. Okay.

IRENE. I just wasn't quite –

NED. It's fine.

IRENE. No, I want to hear it.

NED. I just –

IRENE. I do I want to, I really do.

NED. I don't –

IRENE. So they went to New Orleans, and there was a fever.

NED. The yellow fever.

IRENE. It sounds awful.

NED. It was.

(Silence. He drinks.)

IRENE. And then there was something else?

NED. Something else?

IRENE. You said somebody went someplace?

NED. Indianapolis! They lived there for a long time, and you know, they thought they had left all this hardship behind them.

IRENE. Uh-huh.

NED. And then there was, the flu pandemic.

IRENE. The flu?

NED. You don't know about the flu?

IRENE. You mean like the flu, flu?

NED. Well, it wasn't like any flu. It was like, it killed a third of the planet.

IRENE. Really.

NED. You don't know about this?

IRENE. I heard about it, I think.

NED. This was back in 1918.

IRENE. Oh.

NED. It was a pandemic. That's what they call it when so many people die all over the planet, it's a pandemic –

IRENE. I didn't know that.

NED. It was a terrible disease.

> *(There is a pause at this.* **IRENE** *keeps eating french fries.* **LILA** *enters behind the bar, checks in with people, if they want another drink.)*

People would start bleeding from your nose and your eyes, and then you would be dead in hours, in screaming agony.

IRENE. Ohhhh.

NED. Millions of people, dying this way. Whole families wiped out, there was no place to bury them all. More people died from the flu, than died from World War I.

IRENE. Really.

NED. My family was already – it was – and then to get hit, they were like, nothing was left. No one.

IRENE. Except you!

NED. I wasn't born yet.

IRENE. No, I know.

NED. Well, then what do you mean, except me?

IRENE. I just meant, how could your whole family be wiped out, if you're here? I mean, if they were all wiped out, how would you be here?

NED. Look, the point is, there was tremendous devastation.

IRENE. A lot of people died.

NED. That's right, a lot of people died. So many people, it's just, it's not war that worries me about the human race. That's not really that bad, if you think about it.

IRENE. "War" isn't – "that bad" –

NED. No it isn't and here's why. Here's why. War is a natural cleansing.

IRENE. A "cleansing"?

NED. That's right, it's a human need, men need war –

IRENE. Men "need" war –

NED. Let me finish! Men clearly need war, it's built into their nature, it's an essential part of the DNA of the race, because the race, people, understand that this planet is only so big, it's not big enough for all of us, we aren't meant to live all crowded on top of each other and we have to take care of our own excesses. We have to purge, get rid of the extra people.

IRENE. Extra people.

NED. It's violent, and unconscious, but human.

IRENE. So is that what Hitler was doing with the Holocaust, "purging" the extra –

NED. That's exactly what –

IRENE. And that's okay?

NED. I didn't say it was okay –

IRENE. You did say it was okay, just like three seconds ago –

NED. What I said was it didn't worry me –

IRENE. Well it fucking worries me, and this conversation fucking worries me –

NED. No let me finish. What worries me, what really worries me is not what man does to man.

IRENE. Or what man does to woman.

NED. That's not what I'm talking about –

IRENE. I'm so aware –

NED. What WORRIES me is what tiny tiny organisms do. To man. Organisms that have no consciousness, or need or desire, organisms that barely exist themselves. But which can can can sweep over the planet, just like like air. Literally! And they can cause such utter, and it's happened, historically, I mean, I didn't even tell you about the bubonic plague, what a holy mess that was in the Middle Ages, just like once a year it would sweep through Europe and take out a quarter of the population. The rats carried it. But the others, yellow fever and influenza and and cholera, smallpox, that stuff is just in the air we breathe. And it's coming again, you know just historically there is no way to stop it, that's why people get so nervous when there's just a moment like SARS? Or the bird flu? All those monkeys, in Washington. Not to mention the very near miss we just got through. The reason those moments are so terrifying is that people know what could happen, in the world we live in now, the air we breathe touches the air that EVERYONE breathes, and people, borders are so porous now. The planet is smaller. The disease that is in one place reaches another so quickly. And the next pandemic, it will kill billions. BILLIONS. And we're not set up to handle something like that and that'll be it. All men will die.

> *(By this point everyone else in the bar is listening.)*

IRENE. You know, this is actually, this is not a good date.

NED. I'm sorry.

IRENE. I mean, what the FUCK.

NED. I'm not making any of this up.

IRENE. Who gives a shit? We're on a fucking date, you moron. This is a DATE, this isn't you know, some lecture series that I signed up for about global carnage.

NED. I thought you were interested.

IRENE. You didn't – think – I was interested, I clearly WASN'T interested, I'm not even not interested, I'm offended –

NED. You're offended?

IRENE. That's right I'm offended. What horseshit. Men need war? War is OKAY? Slaughtering millions of women and children IS just something MEN need to do to BLOW OFF STEAM?

> *(The argument heats up; they speak on top of each other.)*

NED. I didn't say that.

IRENE. Yes you did, you sat here and said –

NED. What I said –

IRENE. You said –

NED. I was, let me at least defend myself –

> *(They are completely speaking at the same time now.)*

IRENE. You SAID that it was a natural need for men to go to war and slaughter women and children and that you didn't worry about that because a couple of tiny bacteria are more dangerous –

NED. I am, you can't just put words in my mouth. You are putting a moral judgement –

IRENE. Than war, bacteria are more dangerous –

NED. On what was – I'm sorry you have to at least let me explain!

IRENE. More dangerous bacteria are more dangerous than than Hitler which is offensive, honestly –

NED. You, could you please –

IRENE. And if I'm not giving you a chance to explain it's because I don't want to hear you explain –

NED. This is, if you want to talk about what I said I am happy to do that BUT THIS IS UNFAIR!

IRENE. Unfair. You think I'm being "unfair" –

NED. Well, you're just yelling at me and and and distorting, I was trying to make a point –

IRENE. I am not yelling or distorting. I sat here and listened to your utter BULLSHIT for –

NED. It isn't bullshit, it's okay you may not LIKE the fact that men go to war, which wasn't even the point of the discussion –

IRENE. What I don't LIKE is that men go to war and MURDER women and children and then act like, "Oh sorry couldn't help that that's just who we are."

NED. It doesn't matter if you like it or not –

IRENE. "Oh sorry can't quite stop ourselves from murdering people."

NED. War is existentially different from murder –

IRENE. Don't try to make some lame point about that doesn't matter WOMEN DON'T DO THAT EITHER –

NED. Women don't murder?

IRENE. No we don't.

NED. I think you do.

IRENE. Oh look at the statistics.

NED. Women murder men all the time, women are as capable of murder –

IRENE. Women hardly murder men all the time and yes we ARE as capable of murder but we don't do it because we're not MURDERERS!

NED. Okay I never said –

IRENE. And women don't –

NED. That all men are murderers, that is not –

IRENE. Go to war – women don't go to war because war is immoral –

NED. You are really twisting –

IRENE. And if men NEED war so badly –

NED. You are twisting, this isn't even the point I was trying to –

IRENE. You NEED to go to war, then I don't understand why you don't leave us out of it –

NED. This is so off what I was talking about –

IRENE. And you can leave us out of of all your, your child prostitution –

NED. Could we could we okay –

IRENE. Because that's another thing that women don't need –

NED. Okay –

IRENE. Sex slaves, something else we wouldn't –

NED. Women participate in in in –

IRENE. Pornography, how many women are out there going, "Oh gotta get me some internet porn, I love watching someone shoving his giant dick into some bitch's pussy"–

NED. OKAY. OKAY. I GOT IT. OKAY.

> (**IRENE** *suddenly stops. There is a sullen silence. The others watch.*)

I think we're just not really hearing each other on this. The yin/yang of the planet is a littttle off these days, I'd say. Let's talk about something else.

> (*Then:*)

How about sports?

> (**IRENE** *throws her fries at him. He reacts, startled, and then she throws his beer at him.*)
>
> (*Blackout.*)

Scene Two

> (**PATRICK** *and* **BARRY** *laughing their heads off,*
> *telling the story to* **NICK.**)

NICK. She said WHAT?

PATRICK. She said, "I love watching someone stick his dick
into some bitch's pussy."

LILA. *(Overlap, entering from kitchen.)* Do not repeat that
could you please not repeat it!

> *(But she is cheerful. The story is that good.)*

NICK. Wow, what? She said –

LILA. Yes, she said this crazy nasty thing, and then she
threw her french fries at him.

PATRICK. And then she threw her BEER at him!

LILA. It wasn't her beer; it was his beer.

PATRICK. It was her beer. I thought she was going to hit
him with her chair.

> *(He picks up a chair and starts to swing it*
> *around.)*

LILA. *(Laughing.)* She didn't!

NICK. Holy shit!

PATRICK. Seriously this woman was fucking BUTCH. We
all thought she was going to take him DOWN.

> *(He sets down the chair.)*

LILA. She was mad; she wasn't "butch."

NICK. Did she hit him?

LILA. No, she threw his beer at him and left!

NICK. Did he follow her?

PATRICK. Would you?

LILA. Come on, he was the one, he was being such a jerk.

PATRICK. HE was being a jerk? She threw a beer at him!

LILA. Did you tell him about the argument?

PATRICK. Yes, I told him –

(*He is distracted now. He is looking at the edge of the bartop.*)

LILA. (*This is a great story.*) They were having this argument. Actually, it wasn't actually even an argument.

NICK. So why'd she throw her fucking beer at him?

LILA. He was giving this LECTURE about, I don't know, something. Death.

NICK. He was giving a lecture about death?

BARRY. It was about disease.

NICK. Oh that's much better.

BARRY. It was about the flu and ebola and bubonic plague.

NICK. Whoa. Really?

BARRY. He was just talking.

LILA. He was talking about death, and then he said that war was okay and it pissed her off.

PATRICK. He never said that war was okay.

LILA. You couldn't really hear what they were saying, they were over there.

BARRY. I could hear what they were saying.

PATRICK. It doesn't matter what they were saying.

LILA. How could it not matter?

PATRICK. I mean she's the one who threw the punch.

LILA. She didn't throw a punch.

PATRICK. She threw her food at him. And her beer.

LILA. It wasn't her beer! Women don't drink beer! Women drink white wine! They don't drink beer.

NICK. Some women drink beer.

LILA. And some men drink white wine!

PATRICK. Fags.

LILA. Stop stop stop.

PATRICK. You're the one started making stereotypical accusations.

LILA. I did not!

PATRICK. You said –

LILA. I said she wasn't drinking the beer, which she wasn't –

PATRICK. But that's not the point!

LILA. *(Overlap.)* And then you said –

PATRICK. *(Overlap.)* Because I was trying to –

LILA. *(Overlap.)* You said it didn't MATTER what he said because she threw a punch which she didn't –

NICK. *(Overlap.)* Guys guys –

PATRICK. *(Overlap.)* Make a point that – could I please – excuse me, could I please – because you're lucky nothing got hurt. That bartop is valuable is all I'm saying.

LILA. *(Overlap.)* He was being ridiculous, going on and on about stuff that was frankly offensive and she was reacting to that, because it upset her and I could see why it –

PATRICK. *(Overlap.)* She was physically reactive and your property was in – I am trying to make a point here! Could you could you – I AM MAKING A POINT!

LILA. You aren't making a point, you're just yelling and trying to drown me out, when I'm trying to make a point.

    (A beat.)

NICK. Geez. This is like cable news.

LILA. The fact is he WAS saying offensive things and they clearly didn't know each other very well and she finally lost her temper!

PATRICK. My point being –

LILA. You can't blame her for losing her temper, he was –

PATRICK. MY POINT BEING, she was the one who started using language and throwing things. She was all, "Men love war, men are killers," and the fact is, she's the one who threw her fucking french fries at him, and said, you know. She used strong language. And this is your bar, your property, which could have gotten dinged, there was no respect for that.

NICK. *(Intervening.)* So what was he saying that pissed her off so much?

PATRICK. Who cares?

BARRY. No, it was interesting. He was all, he was worried, actually, about you know, disease and the end of the world. So he was kind of telling stories about that.

NICK. The end of the world?

LILA. Right? It was so dreary.

BARRY. No, he was knowledgable. I think he was a, you know, he was like a doctor or something.

LILA. He wasn't a doctor.

BARRY. Yes he was. He talked about how diseases are more dangerous than war, and that, it was interesting what he was saying. That sure you can get upset about war –

LILA. You "can" get upset about war?

NICK. Let him finish!

BARRY. But it's really scarier that you know, there's so many diseases out there that really don't, they just kill people and wreck, you know. Everything. And how we don't, the whole planet, these things come along, in history, this is true, like a disease comes along, like bubonic plague, and just wipes everyone out and that is worse than anything. Because it's like the hand of God, coming down, just taking us off the earth. And that's worse than man doing it to himself.

NICK. This guy was saying this to his date, in a bar? I would have thrown my beer at him too.

(**LILA** *gives him a high five.*)

PATRICK. No no no –

BARRY. He was okay, he was just sad.

NICK. He sounds like a drip.

BARRY. He was sad. It was sad what he was talking about, there's no question, but he wasn't mean or anything. I mean, you understood why she might be frustrated –

PATRICK. I didn't understand!

BARRY. Well, I didn't either, because he was, you know, he was a sad doctor, I thought he was interesting.

LILA. Why did you think he was a doctor again?

BARRY. He kept talking about diseases.

PATRICK. Pandemic.

BARRY. Pandemic. That's right, he talked about "pandemic," that's, normal people don't say things like that. He said "influenza pandemic."

> *(He is impressed with this, but the conversation has cooled considerably, people losing their interest. **LILA** is checking the stock behind the bar.)*

LILA. Are we out of Dewar's?

NICK. We can't be, I just ordered a new case.

> *(He goes behind the bar.)*

LILA. I can't find the Belvedere either.

NICK. Now that we're not restocking, remember? It's too expensive.

LILA. People ask for it.

NICK. People?

> *(He looks around. But for them, the place is deserted.)*

LILA. Somebody asked for it – last week, somebody asked for it.

NICK. Who? Don't answer that. Whoever it was, if they ever come back, they can make do with the Absolut.

LILA. Come on. There's no top-end anything, and people are, there's a whole new mixology thing going on now, people are looking for fancy drinks now. It looks like a college bar back here, beer and bad wine and, you know. Bottom shelf. That's not the kind of bar we are. Get some top-drawer vodka, would you? This is a gorgeous place, people come in here, they want to have an experience.

NICK. You can't have an experience with Absolut?

PATRICK. I've had some amazing experiences with a bottle of Absolut. I don't remember any of them. But I definitely had them. Nick had them too. In this very bar! Those three –

NICK. I don't remember.

PATRICK. I don't remember either. But those were some good times. Lost to us forever now.

(BARRY *and* NICK *laugh.* LILA *rolls her eyes.*)

LILA. I'm going to check the freezer, see how that's holding up.

(*She goes.* NICK *grabs a bottle of Jack Daniels and tops off* PATRICK *and* BARRY.)

PATRICK. You didn't talk to her.

NICK. I'm going to.

PATRICK. Is there a problem?

NICK. I need the right –

(*They start to talk on top of each other.*)

PATRICK. Because if there's a problem –

NICK. There's no problem!

PATRICK. This is not a fluid situation, these people are really in the market –

NICK. I realize that but I –

PATRICK. I told them how gorgeous it was, the mirror and the bartop, but they need to be able to come look at it and that's partly, last night if that woman had dinged something up I don't know –

NICK. But that didn't happen –

PATRICK. But it could happen. Every single day something could happen, that would affect the value –

NICK. Could you –

PATRICK. I'm just saying you don't want to do that because the numbers –

NICK. Could you let me –

PATRICK. The numbers they are tossing around are –

NICK. I know, could you let me –

PATRICK. Just crazy. But they want to see it now.

NICK. You just brought this to me not three days ago, nothing happens that fast –

PATRICK. Oh yes things do happen that fast. Last night –

NICK. I wasn't here last night –

PATRICK. If you were, you would have seen, it was an explosion and this is an explosion too, or it could be. It's happening, you could make it happen, but you know if you wait like forever it's not going to happen. That's all I'm saying.

NICK. This place has been in her family for a long time. There's a lot of history here, you can't just step all over that –

PATRICK. Hey listen history is gone. It's gone, it's not the present –

NICK. You can't just say that.

PATRICK. I can just say that. It's the easiest thing in the world to just say that. History is just weight. This place is weight.

NICK. She's not going to see it that way.

PATRICK. The way she sees it isn't making sense anymore. It doesn't matter how long it's been, sometimes things are around so long that they don't make any sense, and we don't live in a world where that's allowed. History is just too expensive! I mean this place is gorgeous. Anyone can see that. But it's past its prime. Anyone can see that too. You come here, you have a few drinks and a few laughs, it's great. But in the morning the joint doesn't look so hot.

BARRY. Neither do you for that matter.

PATRICK. Neither do any of us.

NICK. I think I look pretty good.

PATRICK. Keep telling yourself that.

> (**NICK** *is pouring them all drinks. He glances toward the kitchen, nervous, pours himself a shot as well.*)

Listen, we've all had things happen to us here, events, conversations, disasters, good things too, you met Lila here and fell in love, there's no denying that important things happened here. But in another way, another way to look at it is, they didn't happen here at all. They didn't happen in this place. They happened inside you. But this place is evaporating. It's evaporating. Because there's no money. And that's all America is now. They build a TGI Fridays a mile down the road, we know places like that are for shit but no one cares. They're loud, they're noisy, the drinks suck but they got commercials on the television and they're in the middle of a mall where it's all money and food courts and multiplexes and you can't even, the light is so bad in those places. The food. It's like all anyone eats is, you can't eat it, that stuff, you can't eat it. Phony cheese dip that someone sticks in a microwave and then they pour it on a Tostito. It's worse than Velveeta, that stuff. Who thought they could make cheese worse than Velveeta? I don't know. I don't know.

NICK. You okay?

PATRICK. I'm fine. I'm fine. Don't mistake me. This place, is like holy to me. You guys being here, all these years, just having drinks and holy shit the shit that used to go down. Nicky, you remember –

BARRY. Okay here it comes.

PATRICK. *(To* **BARRY.***)* You ever hear the story –

BARRY. I heard a lot of stories –

PATRICK. Nicky, that time when Lila's dad got sick, I was tending bar –

NICK. *I* was tending bar. You were –

PATRICK. You were hanging out trying to get Lila's attention.

NICK. She was nineteen –

BARRY. I bet she was pretty –

PATRICK. At nineteen, she was jailbait.

NICK. Wait wait wait –

PATRICK. That's not what I'm talking about –

NICK. She was never jailbait!

PATRICK. So he had been sniffing around, no question, and Lila's dad went into the hospital for something –

NICK. It was a heart attack! He had a total, whatever that is when eight valves shut down –

PATRICK. So I'm in charge of the bar –

BARRY. That seems like a bad idea –

PATRICK. It was.

NICK. He was drunk the whole time. I was working the bar.

PATRICK. You were hanging out and flirting with your future.

NICK. Oh man it was crazy back then, there was nothing all the way out here, no mall, just a couple of, the shops over on Curson –

BARRY. This is before the mall?

PATRICK. Yeah, yeah. And every night, it's just the two of us tending bar –

NICK. I worked the bar, he hung out and drank –

PATRICK. And it was getting wilder and wilder, things were completely out of control, Lila was at the hospital day and night and it was –

NICK. There were no controls –

PATRICK. Anyway one night these hookers –

BARRY. Hookers? There were hookers in here?

NICK. The place was lit up. Every kind of everything was in here.

PATRICK. So they're just fucking screaming at each other.

NICK. One of them hits the other, tries to yank her hair out.

BARRY. Come on –

NICK. Serious –

PATRICK. So we're just shouting at them and they completely ignore us.

NICK. IgNORE us.

PATRICK. And it turns into an utter shitstorm and the cops show up and we have to stand there and admit that we couldn't control a pair of fucking hookers.

(**NICK** *is laughing.*)

PATRICK. And the cops were pissed. They were ready to shutter us for disturbing the peace, whatever. So I'm thinking no. They are not shutting my friend's bar down because the two of us clowns couldn't get a pair of hookers to stop screaming at each other.

BARRY. You know, I have not heard this one.

PATRICK. So there's this guy who's drinking here at the time. His name was Indian Dave.

BARRY. Was he an Indian?

PATRICK. Yes he was an Indian.

NICK. He was an Indian.

PATRICK. And he was, you didn't fuck with this guy.

BARRY. Not with a name like "Indian Dave."

PATRICK. Plus he was like six-foot-six, big, long hair, he'd come in and play Sam Cooke on the jukebox.

BARRY. Hang on. That jukebox worked?

PATRICK. Everything worked. So I said to this guy, could you just sit here at the bar, and – what did he drink?

NICK. Seagram's VO with Coke.

PATRICK. That's right, Seagram's and Coke, and we said, basically, you can sit here and drink all night, every night, but if something happens we need you to take care of it. And he said –

NICK. "Sure."

PATRICK. He just kind of nodded, sure that sounded –

NICK. So every night for it must've been weeks –

PATRICK. At least –

NICK. He just sat there and whenever anyone acted up he would stand up and grab them by the neck and force them out the door. It worked like a dream. So we were –

PATRICK. And then one night all of a sudden, the cops are back. They're out there, the red and blue lights going, and he looks out the window, reaches into his shirt and says to me –

NICK. "Handle this."

BARRY. Oh oh –

PATRICK. Handle this! And then he throws this thing to me, I didn't know what it was, I just tossed it under the bar –

NICK. The cops are right on top of us.

PATRICK. And they drag him out, and they're talking to him out there and one of them is waiting by the bartop and I'm like, is something wrong, Officer? And he says, "Has that guy given you any trouble?" And I'm, no, no. So he leaves. And this friend of his is there.

BARRY. Friend of –

PATRICK. Dave's, Indian Dave's.

BARRY. That guy had friends?

PATRICK. So I say, "What was in that thing that he tossed to me." I'm looking under the bartop now. And he says, "That was his balloon of heroin. And his needle. He's going to want that shit back when he gets back here."

(A silence.)

NICK. And then we couldn't find it.

(He starts to laugh.)

BARRY. You couldn't find –

NICK. The heroin!

PATRICK. It was gone.

BARRY. Where did it go?

PATRICK. It was stuck down there.

BARRY. How could it get stuck.

NICK. There's like a space, between the bartop and the floor. Of course we didn't know that.

PATRICK. You couldn't see it, from the angle so no shit, it looked like the thing had just disappeared.

NICK. It just –

PATRICK. *(Laughing.)* So we were tearing up the floor –

NICK. *(Laughing.)* The baseboard, around the –

PATRICK. And you could see it like down in the earth down there –

NICK. *(Laughing.)* And there was no way to get it.

(They were laughing.)

PATRICK. No way.

NICK. It was stuck.

BARRY. So it's still there?

NICK. It could be.

PATRICK. Yeah, it could be.

BARRY. So what happened when he came back?

NICK. He didn't. He moved on.

(They think about that.)

PATRICK. So let me tell you something. Nothing that interesting ever happened in a TGI Fridays. They're all eating Velveeta and there's no action. Those places, they are not as good as this place, not in a million years. But the rules changed.

You didn't ask for the world to change. But there's no fighting it, it's going to happen whether you like it or not. To stand up in this world, to be a man, to have a life? You have to take what's yours and live in the present, and you have to have money to do that. And you keep your memories. But you don't kid yourself, that that's what they are.

(He pours himself a drink. **BARRY** *too.)*

BARRY. I don't know. It's awful nice here. He's right, it's good to have money. But this place is nice.

PATRICK. Don't tell him that.

BARRY. I'll tell him what I want to tell him.

PATRICK. You're not thinking what's best for him.

BARRY. Yeah but who knows what's best for anybody. This bar he has, this is the one thing he has. What if it don't work out, when he sells it? Then he has nothing.

PATRICK. He has his life.

BARRY. He has that whether or not he sells The Nest.

PATRICK. Now you're confusing the issue.

BARRY. I'm not confusing anything, I'm just talking.

NICK. He's right.

PATRICK. He's not right!

BARRY. I don't have to be right. I'm just talking.

PATRICK. So now you don't want to do it? You don't want to do this now? Is that what you're telling me. You want things to stay as they are?

(*A beat.*)

NICK. I'd rather kill myself.

(*They think about this.*)

PATRICK. Okay. She's going to be a little reactive to the whole idea, that's to be expected.

NICK. That's all it is.

PATRICK. But these people are serious.

NICK. And they said it was worth a lot.

(*He looks at the bar. The bartop and the mirror behind are really quite beautiful.*)

PATRICK. They have to send somebody to come look at it. Ascertain how old it is and such.

NICK. It's old, I can tell you that myself. Eighteen sixty something, it's been here –

PATRICK. (*Overlap.*) I know but they can't just take my word on it. This guy is flying himself in, from Chicago.

NICK. (*Overlap.*) For at least that long, maybe eighteen seventy something –

PATRICK. (*Overlap.*) My point being they're serious, they're really fucking serious –

NICK. (*Overlap.*) There are papers around here somewhere –

PATRICK. (*Overlap.*) I'm just telling you. They're sending this guy in specially to take a look and Lila's going to have to be cool with that.

(**LILA** *enters carrying an armful of stuff from the freezer.*)

LILA. Cool with what?

PATRICK. Nothing.

NICK. Nothing.

LILA. Okay you're both acting completely suspicious now.

NICK. It's not anything.

PATRICK. It's nothing.

LILA. This is supposed to reassure me?

(**NICK** *kisses her.*)

NICK. I'll tell you about it later. What's this?

LILA. Those steaks we got in the freezer.

(*She knocks it on the counter. It is rock solid.*)

Appetizing, right? Anybody want one?

NICK. No no no no no!

LILA. They've been in there –

NICK. Yeah but they're good –

BARRY. You're giving these away?

NICK. She's not giving away steaks.

(*He tries to take them back.*)

PATRICK. I'll take one.

NICK. These are fine, they're going back in the freezer, get your hands off that.

PATRICK. Lila's giving it to me as a present.

NICK. And I'm taking it back.

LILA. We're not going to sell them, Nick! I thought it was a terrific idea when you brought it up but it didn't work and now I want to get rid of them before they hit their expiration date. After that we'd just have to toss them and that's a waste.

BARRY. How would you sell them? Like, if someone came in and said they wanted a steak wouldn't you have to say oh we have them but they're ice cubes.

NICK. (*Annoyed.*) You defrost them in the microwave.

LILA. Except no one ever orders steak. They should, but they don't. Take 'em.

(*She hands one each to* **BARRY** *and* **PATRICK** *and turns to take the rest back to the kitchen.*)

NICK. Just don't – give it to the soup kitchen.

LILA. Someone's got to eat it.

NICK. That's expensive steak!

LILA. And the homeless people will feel like it's Christmas.

BARRY. Better than Christmas.

LILA. There's nothing better than Christmas.

BARRY. Memorial Day.

LILA. Memorial Day, are you kidding?

BARRY. It's fun; you get to barbecue.

NICK. I didn't pay however much I paid for that stuff just to feed it to some homeless person! You can give some to Barry and Patrick, but I'm not giving it to the homeless.

> (**LILA** *looks at him, annoyed. Picks up the steaks and turns.*)

LILA. Okay fine. But let me tell you something. Whatever you and your friends think I "have" to be cool with? I don't have to be cool with it.

> (*She goes. They look at each other.*)

NICK. She'll be fine with it. She's fine. She's fine. She's going to be fine.

LILA. (*Re-entering.*) I wouldn't be so sure of that.

> (**BARRY** *and* **PATRICK** *go "Whooaaaa."*)

Don't do that either.

> (**MARGO** *enters.*)

Hey, how's it going?

MARGO. I need a drink. I need the biggest glass of Chardonnay you ever poured. Can I have a glass of Chardonnay in one of those huge wine glasses, can you just find one of those big, you're supposed to use them for red in fancy restaurants, do you have anything like that? Or something more the size of a chip bowl. Hey, Nicky. So gorgeous. Why are all the good men taken?

PATRICK. I'm not taken. Barry's not taken.

MARGO. Barry, you're not taken?

BARRY. Not presently.

MARGO. That's good to know.

> (**LILA** *keeps looking, pulls out a big bowl of a glass from a bottom shelf.*)

LILA. What about this.

MARGO. Now you're talking. What a day. Those FUCKERS. I mean, seriously those motherfuckers, they are, now they're doing the programming meetings at lunch but I don't get invited to lunch. Can you believe that? It's so fifties. I want to kill them, I swear I have terrible fantasies. You know what I think, the solution is about guns? To give them to women.

No kidding, make it illegal for men to have them but sell them to women, make it a law that women have to have a concealed weapon on them at all times. That would even things up. That would get them to act like adults.

PATRICK. Oh that's real mature.

MARGO. Mature? Did you just accuse me of being immature?

PATRICK. I'm just saying, guns are nothing to joke about.

MARGO. Who's joking? I think this is a fantastic idea. Those women in India and Pakistan who keep getting raped and murdered, they could use a few weapons if you ask me.

PATRICK. What they do halfway around the world is their business, I'm not taking that on. Although I think that makes a good point, what you just said.

Those women in India and Pakistan, they have a rough time of it. They have to work just to get an education, or ride a bus or you know, all sorts of things.

MARGO. Those blankets they have to wear on their heads.

PATRICK. That's right, they have to wear blankets.

MARGO. So I would have something to complain about if they were trying to make me wear a blanket on my head?

PATRICK. I'm just saying, it gives perspective.

MARGO. Doesn't it piss you off, when they wear those things here?

LILA. People have their own customs.

MARGO. That's very enlightened of you, because I want to yell at them. Like, if you want to let them make you wear blankets on your head over there in the Middle East be my guest. But do not come all the way to America and then wear those fucking blankets. You might give these clowns ideas. Seriously. These guys at my work would love to put a blanket over my head. I'm watching my back all the time down there. It's like high school. It's like Lord of the Flies.

BARRY. There were no girls in Lord of the Flies.

MARGO. That's right, there weren't, because they ATE them.

  (*She laughs and drinks.*)

LILA. Tell Nick what happened last night.

MARGO. Last night, what happened last night?

LILA. Last night, those two –

MARGO. Oh, you mean those two on the setup?

NICK. It was a setup?

MARGO. It was like a computer date or something. They didn't know each other.

BARRY. How do you know that?

MARGO. How do I know that? I just do, I was sitting right next to them, they didn't know each other.

BARRY. I was closer and I didn't hear anything about a computer date.

MARGO. I was closer.

BARRY. Yeah but I could hear them. I mean you were closer but I could hear them. I thought he was kind of interesting, the things he was saying I mean.

MARGO. All that stuff about blowing up the planet?

BARRY. He wasn't talking about blowing up the planet.

MARGO. He totally was, he was all –

BARRY. No no no he was making a point about war, about how we're in control of war so –

MARGO. We're in control of war?

LILA. Don't get distracted.

MARGO. No seriously –

BARRY. That's what he said, and it was a good point I thought. That war is something we do but you know there are all these bacteria out there that we have no control over and that could end up, we don't have any power over that, and it could destroy us.

MARGO. *(Getting revved up.)* Okay okay. Okay FIRST of all –

LILA. No –

MARGO. We are NOT in control of war, it sounds idiotic whenever you guys say that –

PATRICK. You guys, what is that supposed to mean?

MARGO. Women don't start wars, suck it up. SECOND of all, once you're in a war, you are not and I repeat not in control of it. So that whole thing you just said is stupid.

PATRICK. I didn't say anything!

MARGO. Third of all – I can't think of third of all. Can I have some more of this?

LILA. *(Pouring.)* We don't need to have the fight all over again –

MARGO. We might need to have the fight all over again. These clowns clearly missed the whole point of the fight –

BARRY. It wasn't really a fight.

MARGO. It was totally a fight!

LILA. Yeah but I just wanted you to tell Nick about it.

NICK. They already told me.

LILA. They didn't tell you the right way.

*(Both **PATRICK** and **BARRY** start to protest.)*

PATRICK. I told you the way I heard it, you can't ask me to tell you something I didn't hear –

BARRY. *(Simultaneous.)* They were in the middle of a really interesting discussion / is what I said. I didn't think it was a fight, I thought it was a discussion.

MARGO. *(Picking up on "discussion.")* Okay that I can set you straight on, if they told you these two were having a "discussion" that is not what was going on.

Because who knows what that guy was on about, he was all worried about, it was like he had read some book or watched a movie even, there was some movie out there a while ago, about what would happen if everyone got some horrible disease and the whole planet died except for six people. What was the name of that movie. Andromeda Strain?

BARRY. That was like sixty years ago. How old are you?

MARGO. How "old" am I? Did you say that? Forget it, I'm not dating you.

BARRY. I'm just saying, it wasn't Andromeda Strain. No wait, I know this movie. Charlton Heston was in it.

MARGO. Charlton Heston? How old are you?

BARRY. Everybody dies! Everybody gets sick and dies, or turns into zombies.

NICK. Planet of the Apes.

LILA. Oh my god we loved that.

NICK. Rise of the Planet of the Apes. And they didn't turn into apes, they WERE apes.

PATRICK. Omega Man. That's not what you're thinking about, you're thinking about the remake. Will Smith was in it, with this dog. There's this doctor who thinks she's cured cancer, and she's kind of smug about it, and the next thing you know the whole human race is gone. Or, they're turned into zombies.

MARGO. She's "kind of smug about it"? Wouldn't you be, if you cured cancer?

PATRICK. I'm just describing the movie.

MARGO. So if a man cured cancer, would you accuse him of being smug about it?

PATRICK. This is not some huge feminist attack, I'm just describing the movie!

LILA. Okay but we were talking about –

MARGO. *(Overlap.)* We're talking about disease movies! There was a total disease movie out there, like just last year. Two years ago. Everyone got sick and died. It was just a few years ago. I didn't see it but it was out just like last year and it was about you know, what he was talking about. Everybody getting sick. No zombies.

BARRY. No, she's right she's right. I saw that.

MARGO. Was it any good?

BARRY. It was a little boring.

MARGO. What was it called?

BARRY. I can't remember. Something really specific. Like, "Everybody Gets Sick and Dies."

(They laugh.)

PATRICK. He wasn't talking about a movie.

LILA. Oh come on we finally agreed on something.

PATRICK. He was talking about his family, about coming to America.

LILA. He was?

PATRICK. Yeah, he was trying to make a point about how his whole family immigrated to America.

LILA. Okay now we're into crazy land because I don't remember anything about immigration. Immigration? They were talking about –

PATRICK. You were in the kitchen, so you missed this part.

BARRY. That's right, you were in the kitchen!

MARGO. *(To NICK.)* They're right, she was in the kitchen.

NICK. What was she doing there?

LILA. I was putting in an order of fries and chicken fingers, for Barry.

PATRICK. She burned 'em.

NICK. She BURNED them.

(*This amuses him.*)

LILA. I was busy cleaning up after these two nuts left, I put the order in while they were I don't know, I guess they were discussing immigration, and then they threw their beer and fries everywhere and I was cleaning up and I forgot about the chicken fingers because I was cleaning up.

BARRY. It was just her throwing. He didn't throw anything.

LILA. I don't care who threw it –

PATRICK. SHE threw it. SHE threw it, after she was all "men start war" but she threw the fries AND the beer.

LILA. But I had to clean it up.

MARGO. It's true. War starts, people die, women have to clean up the mess.

PATRICK. And women do start wars.

MARGO. Women do not start wars.

BARRY. Margaret Thatcher.

MARGO. One woman.

BARRY. Indira Gandhi.

MARGO. Okay.

BARRY. Helen of Troy.

MARGO. She didn't start that.

BARRY. Cleopatra.

MARGO. This is stupid.

NICK. It is stupid. I want to hear some more about how she burned all the food.

LILA. I did not burn it.

BARRY. It was crispy. I didn't mind.

PATRICK. My god they were like little black, this frozen block of meat is more edible than those things were.

NICK. You wouldn't eat it like that. Let me cook it for you. Come on.

PATRICK. Are you going to charge me for cooking it?

NICK. Am I going to charge you for a steak dinner? Yes, I'm going to charge you for a steak dinner.

PATRICK. Well then I'm just going to take it home.

NICK. Give it back.

PATRICK. She gave it to me! It was a present.

MARGO. Who got a present, I want a present.

NICK. No more presents. I want to hear about the immigration debate.

MARGO. It wasn't about immigration, that's not what he was talking about. It was more, my poor family, like all these people have been dead for two hundred years, and he was all upset about that.

LILA. Why?

MARGO. Well, exactly. This is why I was on her side. Who gives a shit? She sat there and just listened and listened and it went on forever and then she finally snapped. Which is what happens to women, it really is. And then you guys all say we're crazy. When we're not crazy, we're just tired of listening.

PATRICK. So that makes it okay? She was "tired of listening," so it's okay for her to to throw her french fries at him? And maybe you know, potentially damage the bartop?

MARGO. She didn't damage the bartop, did she?

(She goes to examine it.)

PATRICK. I didn't say she did damage it, I said she potentially damaged it.

MARGO. By throwing her french fries?

LILA. It's fine, I cleaned it up.

MARGO. *(Looking.)* This thing is built like a rock.

LILA. It's all that marble. It *is* a rock.

MARGO. Well, anyway. It was all pretty interesting. And then he said this reasonably smart thing about how the yin/yang of the planet is off, which I think is not a bad point –

BARRY. What did that mean?

MARGO. It means – you know, that little thing that fits together, the little –

LILA. It's a little –

NICK. It's like a little drawing –

BARRY. So what's that got to do with –

NICK. It's like a little two parts fit together –

(He is drawing it.)

BARRY. Yeah but –

MARGO. The yin/yang, men and women don't fit together anymore, he sort of was apologizing, and then he wanted to talk about SPORTS.

(She laughs.)

And THAT'S when the fries went EVERYWHERE. Do you have any french fries?

LILA. I do. Do you want a steak?

MARGO. If I wanted a steak I wouldn't come here for it.

(There is a bad pause at this.)

What? Oh, what? I'm just saying, who would come here for a steak? You don't serve steak in bars.

NICK. Yeah. We do. Really good steak, actually.

MARGO. You do?

LILA. We were trying to you know. Get things moving up a notch. People don't want to go out and blow a whole wad on a crazy expensive dinner, what if you can have a nice dinner, in a nice place, that's in the neighborhood, doesn't cost a fortune but is still really good. Like, if your choice is one of these crazy chains, or some other place way too expensive, maybe people would rather go someplace where you can get a good price for a meal and also have the feeling of something better than just corporate bullshit. Like that.

*(**NICK** turns, pours himself a drink.)*

PATRICK. A primo cut. They call it Rock Ribeye.

(He taps it on the bar. It sure sounds like a rock.)

LILA. It's not ribeye, it's filet mignon, it's freeze-dried, and it's delicious. Seriously, it's just like the way they freeze shrimp out on the shrimp boats, you have to freeze it or it'll go bad.

So we just get the meat frozen the same way but you can have a perfectly cooked steak within minutes, rare, medium, medium rare –

MARGO. It's okay, I don't really want a steak. Just some fries. And another one of these.

(*She holds up her glass.*)

NICK. Yeah okay but that's a double, you know that right? That's twice the size of a normal glass of wine, I got to charge you double.

(*He holds up the bottle, waits.*)

MARGO. Yeah, of course. I assumed that.

NICK. So that's four glasses of wine. Would have made sense to just buy the bottle for yourself.

(*He pours.* **MARGO** *sits there, humiliated, then:*)

MARGO. Awesome. My own bottle of wine to suck down. Well and it's been that kind of day. Thanks Nick.

(*She takes the drink.* **LILA** *looks at* **NICK**, *pissed, and goes into the kitchen.* **NICK** *looks after her, what's she mad about?*)

BARRY. I don't disagree with you. I mean, I don't disagree they were not on the same page. I just meant, from what I saw, or heard, more what I heard, because I was a little closer than you, was that he was really trying to communicate something serious. I agree that war is, you know, that's not a, we don't want to talk about war, that's not what the point was. He was more talking about plague. He said pandemic, which is why I thought he's a doctor? You know who uses words like pandemic? But what he was talking about is plague, and how that's, you know, mythic. How that is more like the earth reaching out and killing us. Not even the earth, that's not what I mean. Although why not, you know, why wouldn't the earth want to kill us? We spend enough time trying to kill it. But that's not what he was saying. He was more saying you know, nature, it's bigger than all of us. Or maybe he just read a book about ebola. I read a book about that once, it was scary as shit.

PATRICK. But we're all going to die anyway is the point.

BARRY. It might be, I don't know.

PATRICK. We're all going to die so what's the use of hanging onto something that's dying too.

BARRY. That wasn't his point.

PATRICK. It's my point.

NICK. Okay.

PATRICK. I'm just giving you encouragement. You hang onto something dead, you're going to die too.

NICK. This is encouragement?

PATRICK. It's the truth.

BARRY. Yeah but, you know there's a lot of different truths out there.

PATRICK. No there isn't.

BARRY. Oh yes there is. Every time somebody tells me I got to admit the truth I think okay you're about to tell me sometime that's actually not too far off a lie.

PATRICK. That's not the kind of truth I'm talking about.

BARRY. One time someone called me a liar. Out of nowhere. I leant him money. Not a lot. Well, a lot for me, at the time. And I didn't expect to get it back; you lend somebody money you better know you're never getting it back. So I was okay with that. But then my son had to go and ask for it back. And don't get me wrong, I love him, I am proud of that boy. I don't understand most the words come out of his mouth these days but he's strong in the world. And he said you got to get that money back and he went and asked for it, and the man called me a liar. Said I never gave him the money.

PATRICK. Yeah but he knew he was lying.

BARRY. Did he?

PATRICK. That's not what we're talking about.

BARRY. I know. I just get a little nervous when the words "truth" and "money" start getting tossed around in the same conversation.

PATRICK. This isn't the same conversation, this is about eight conversations.

BARRY. Okay.

PATRICK. You ready?

BARRY. Oh are we going?

PATRICK. We hanging out for something?

BARRY. No, I just, you know. I still have half my drink.

PATRICK. You want to hang out here, that's fine. It's just there's not much going on.

BARRY. Well, but I have half my drink.

PATRICK. That's fine.

BARRY. Okay.

> *(A beat.)*

Okay then! Okay.

> *(**PATRICK** heads for the door. **BARRY** gathers up the frozen steaks and follows him. They go. **NICK** and **MARGO**, alone.)*

MARGO. You know I'm going to take off too. What did you say it was, four glasses of Chardonnay?

NICK. You don't want to finish it?

MARGO. It's fine. This should cover the fries, too.

> *(She puts some money on the bartop and goes.)*

NICK. Oh, Jesus.

> *(But she is gone. He watches the back of her go for a moment, then goes around the front of the bar, considers it. He takes another step back, looks at it from a different angle. Then he goes back to the mirror, investigates the carved frame. **LILA** re-enters.)*

LILA. Where'd everybody go?

NICK. I don't know. They just took off.

LILA. Didn't Margo want her fries?

NICK. No, she changed her mind.

LILA. Gee I wonder why.

(She goes to clean up the bar.)

NICK. Oh what'd I do now?

LILA. This is a bar, Nick. You don't call your customers drunks. You don't do it.

NICK. I didn't call her a drunk.

LILA. You absolutely –

NICK. I said she had to pay for her drinks –

LILA. Why? You don't make your friends pay for their drinks.

NICK. Of course they –

LILA. You topped them off, you –

NICK. Jesus, it's a fucking bar –

LILA. That's right it is and you –

NICK. You're the one giving away steaks!

LILA. Is that what this is about? You're still mad that –

NICK. It's not about anything –

LILA. Nobody is buying those steaks!

NICK. I'm not talking about –

LILA. I thought it was a good idea, obviously –

NICK. I'm not –

LILA. But then it didn't work! People didn't go for it!

NICK. People –

LILA. Maybe if we had added the pot pie and the stuffed shrimp and made it more of a whole menu.

NICK. We didn't have the money to completely rethink the menu.

LILA. But people aren't coming here just for steak.

NICK. People aren't COMING HERE at all.

(A beat.)

LILA. People do come here.

NICK. Oh boy.

LILA. It's slow now. When the mall went up –

NICK. The mall went up seven years ago, we've been fighting this for seven years –

LILA. It hasn't been that bad the whole time –

NICK. Yes it has. Lila it has. When they put the freeway in and the turnoff ended up two miles away in the wrong direction that was the end of everything. We just didn't know it.

LILA. Patrick's got you all tuned up again.

NICK. This isn't about Patrick.

LILA. What's his big idea this time?

NICK. He doesn't have a big idea.

LILA. He always has a big idea. Turn the kitchen into a microbrewery. Update the jukebox! Which by the way it never worked again after he messed with it.

NICK. That's not on him. A lot of people have messed with that jukebox over the years.

LILA. You guys do, you so stick together.

NICK. This isn't about –

LILA. He's so full of shit too. The way he was going on, about did they ding the bartop when they threw their french fries?

NICK. Come on, the bartop is valuable, with all the hand-carving. And the mirror – it's huge, for one thing, and the frame is all hand-carved too.

LILA. It was french fries!

NICK. The point is it's valuable. You can't help but wonder what it's worth.

LILA. It's a family heirloom. It's not worth anything.

NICK. Well, that's – insane.

LILA. I don't mean it's not worth anything, I just mean you can't sell it. You don't sell heirlooms. There's too much history.

NICK. People sell heirlooms all the time.

LILA. You know what I mean. My great-great-great grandfather made this bar –

NICK. Honey, he didn't.

LILA. He carved it himself –

NICK. Listen to me. Somebody carved this bar; there is no question that it's hand-carved. But this story, that some great something carved this bar, you know that's horseshit.

LILA. It's not horseshit. He came here from Germany. He was a clockmaker from Munich –

NICK. *(Overriding her.)* I know the story, that there was some mythic German clockmaker kind of elf person who stowed away on a ship that came to the Statue of Liberty and he said this is my land and I will make a home for myself and carve my life into a bartop and sell beer to the masses and that's America for you, it's your heritage and I understand, I do, but I say this with love, it's horseshit, it's complete – horseshit – that your family has been telling itself for generations here, honey! And that's not to say it's not beautiful horseshit, it is. But you need to trust me on this, Lila. This isn't your family legacy, it's a bar. It's a room, and it's a piece of wood, which people sit around while they get drunk. During Prohibition people sat around this piece of wood and got drunk and murdered each other. It's a bar. It's been here a long time and it's probably worth a lot of money because nobody can do work like that anymore and if they did it would cost hundreds of thousands of dollars.

LILA. Well I think that's an exaggeration.

NICK. It would cost a lot of money and it's worth a lot of money and we need money.

LILA. We're doing fine –

NICK. We're not doing fine. There are things that are true, and things that aren't true. And you're living in a world where those two things are upside down.

LILA. Meaning what?

NICK. Why can't we even discuss this?

LILA. We are discussing it! You're saying you want to sell the bar!

NICK. I am saying that, yes.

LILA. Okay, and I'm saying I don't!

NICK. It's my bar, too.

LILA. What?

NICK. I got twenty-five years of my life in this place. It's my bar, too.

LILA. Well – that's what I'm saying. This is our place. It's our place together. Why would you sell it?

> *(Then:)*

Nick?

> *(He turns away.* **IRENE** *and* **NED** *enter.)*

IRENE. Oh, Hey. Hi!

NED. Remember us?

> *(**NICK** and **LILA** turn and look at them.)*
>
> *(Blackout.)*

ACT TWO

(The bar. **LILA** *and* **NICK**, *telling the story to* **MARGO**, **BARRY**, *and* **PATRICK**. **BARRY** *tries to get the jukebox to work.)*

MARGO. Get out.

LILA. It's true.

MARGO. They came back.

PATRICK. And the bar's still standing?

LILA. They were nice!

PATRICK. Nice?

MARGO. Let her tell it.

BARRY. It doesn't work.

NICK. I told you it doesn't work.

LILA. Their names are Ned Bartish and Irene Colatonio.

PATRICK. Colatonio, that I buy.

LILA. What is that supposed to mean?

PATRICK. She had a temper, you admit yourself she had a temper –

LILA. So "Colatonio" –

MARGO. Don't distract her, tell the story.

NICK. There is no story.

LILA. That is so not true.

BARRY. Leave me alone, I'm good at this.

LILA. First they apologized. They ordered a couple drinks and they apologized like eight times.

NICK. It hasn't worked in twenty years. I should have gotten rid of it by now.

LILA. They were really just nice –

PATRICK. Nice.

MARGO. Let her tell it!

LILA. And laughing, they kept laughing about how hideous they had been –

MARGO. They weren't embarrassed?

LILA. Completely embarrassed, but they came back to apologize, apparently they get into fights like that all the time –

BARRY. I thought it was their first date!

LILA. They've been together for six years.

MARGO. What?

LILA. We were totally wrong about that.

BARRY. Is he a doctor?

LILA. He is not a doctor. He's a graduate student in climatology.

MARGO. ClimaTOLogy?

PATRICK. Hang on.

MARGO. What does she do?

LILA. She teaches at the university too. Are you ready? Women's studies.

MARGO. Yes!

PATRICK. That explains a few things.

BARRY. If they were together for six years how come she kept calling it a date?

LILA. It was their date night. Not a date, date night.

BARRY. That's not what she said.

LILA. That's what she meant.

BARRY. That's not what she said.

LILA. She clearly didn't realize we were taking notes.

PATRICK. She should've, she was loud enough.

MARGO. They were both loud.

PATRICK. She was loud.

MARGO. They were both –

BARRY. He was, he was loud too. He was just kind of sad so he didn't seem as loud.

LILA. So then –

MARGO. Were they still loud?

NICK. They weren't that loud –

MARGO. Really –

LILA. They were kind of loud. They were laughing.

MARGO. They were laughing?

LILA. Yes, I TOLD you, because they had come in and thrown things, they were embarrassed –

PATRICK. Why was HE embarrassed? He didn't throw anything –

MARGO. Yeah but he was loud –

LILA. The point is they were sorry. Really nice and really sorry and pretty interesting honestly. They stayed, ordered a fancy drink. A Sazerac.

BARRY. A what?

LILA. Exactly, we never heard of it either; Nick had to look it up.

NICK. Bourbon, bitters, a twist of lemon.

PATRICK. That's an Old Fashioned.

NICK. I know.

LILA. It was different than an Old Fashioned; he had never even heard of it.

NICK. You're supposed to coat the glass with absinthe.

PATRICK. "Coat the glass"?

NICK. Right?

LILA. So they had that without the coating the glass part, we have to order some absinthe.

(*She goes to write this down.*)

PATRICK. So they had an Old Fashioned.

LILA. AND – they ordered the steak dinner.

(*All react.*)

MARGO. No WAY –

LILA. They did, they ordered it and I made it and they ate it and it was DELICIOUS.

MARGO. They actually had the steak dinner.

NICK. They loved it!

BARRY. What do you get with the steak dinner again?

NICK. You get steak!

LILA. Steak and fries and a house salad.

MARGO. You have a house salad?

LILA. Oh my god. Of COURSE we have a house salad. You can order it alone or with the steak!

MARGO. I never even look at the menu here.

LILA. Well you should because it's about to expand. There's a lot of stuff we can order from the place that does the steaks. Stuffed shrimp, gourmet chicken pot pie –

(She finds the catalogue.)

NICK. As long as it's just you and me here that's not exactly –

LILA. Obviously you wouldn't do it all at once –

BARRY. The steak is good, I had the steak last night, it was, it was really good.

(This lands. They all look at him.)

NICK. You ate the steak?

BARRY. Yeah I took it home and cooked it, it was terrific.

NICK. *(To* **PATRICK.***)* Did you eat your steak?

PATRICK. Yeah.

NICK. How was it?

PATRICK. It was okay.

NICK. OKAY?

PATRICK. It was good.

BARRY. I thought it was good.

LILA. No one ever said the steak wasn't good, it IS good, and they ordered the steak dinner and they had DESSERT. And then they had an after-dinner drink, he had a Glenfiddich and she wanted B&B. But we didn't have that either. So she had an extra glass of Chardonnay. We need to stock B&B.

PATRICK. They sound like total alcoholics.

BARRY. But what did they talk about?

LILA. They talked about how good the food is here, and how beautiful the place is. They're going to tell their friends about it. Their friends from the university, who they think will really appreciate how gorgeous it is and how good the food is. They're telling everybody. And, they left a fantastic tip.

PATRICK. To make up for the fact that they trashed the place the night before.

LILA. And they paid for that, too. They made me add the drinks and fries from the night before, and they added a tip for THAT. They were excellent customers.

(They all think about this.)

BARRY. I don't know. It doesn't sound as lively as the first time they came in.

MARGO. All right, I'm in. I'll have the steak dinner.

LILA. You will?

MARGO. Why not, it sounds great. It comes with fries?

LILA. Steak frite. Fries and a salad.

BARRY. I'll have one too. You in?

PATRICK. Whoa whoa whoa –

BARRY. What? You said it was good. I thought it was terrific.

PATRICK. It's just a little pricey.

BARRY. She gave us two for free last night.

PATRICK. So compared to last night this is pretty pricey.

NICK. It's okay.

LILA. Don't tell him it's okay, if he wants to order the steak dinner, let him!

BARRY. He's having the steak dinner. Make 'em both medium rare.

MARGO. Mine too.

LILA. Three steak dinners. THREE.

(She goes.)

PATRICK. How long does it take? Do you even have that many back there?

NICK. You don't have to have the steak dinner.

MARGO. Come on he does too. Are you going to sit there and let her say that those two nutjobs are better customers than we are? That's three steak frites, and another round.

PATRICK. Are you paying for this?

MARGO. We're all paying for it you freeloader. What's the matter with you?

NICK. He doesn't have to order the steak dinner!

MARGO. Okay okay. Allow me to point something out here. Last night you were all insulted that no one wanted your steaks and now that we're ordering them you're saying no no no. You guys are insane. I mean it. Not one of you knows how to say thank you.

NICK & PATRICK. Thank you.

MARGO. I don't know if the planet was always like this, actually when you look back at the Middle Ages when men were always trying to lop each other's heads off, you suspect that it was.

PATRICK. I'm sorry but you just come out with shit like that and we're the ones who are insane?

MARGO. Honestly, it's the one advantage of being the only woman down at that office. I just sit in the middle of it all and watch. Everything is a test with you clowns. It's exhausting. Even gay men do it. This is what I figured out, this is why it's worse for girls now that gay men are out of the closet.

PATRICK. Oh ho ho. And now you don't like gay men.

MARGO. I like gay men fine. Don't do that.

(It starts to run away from them.)

PATRICK. You just said –

MARGO. I said –

PATRICK. You said it's worse for women that gay men are out of the closet.

MARGO. Yes I did say that because –

PATRICK. So what you're saying –

MARGO. It is worse for women because gay men –

PATRICK. So what you're saying is –

MARGO. Oh come on! I'm not saying everybody, but a bunch of those guys are mad at us because they think they ARE us but if we're there, then that means they AREN'T us, which they don't really want to be us anyway because that's the problem with being a gay man isn't it? It makes you like a WOMAN. It's so stupid.

It's all strong, weak, strong, weak, and if the straight guys are the fucking alpha dogs then women are the bottom of the pack and then everyone in between proves that they're men by kicking the women.

> (**LILA** *re-enters.*)

It's just like all those guys in India who can't get a job and it makes them feel like they're not men so they go out there and rape women. It's just like that.

> (*There is a silence.*)

LILA. I was going to ask what kind of dressing people want on their salads but that doesn't seem like the right question right now.

PATRICK. She hates gay people.

MARGO. I do not hate gay people! I never said that.

PATRICK. She hates men.

MARGO. Oh my god.

LILA. She doesn't hate men.

BARRY. It does sound like you hate gay people.

MARGO. I hate the idiots at my job –

PATRICK. But that's not what you said –

MARGO. They act like I'm a freak and this is my point: They treat me shitty because they don't want to be like me! But they are like me! Why aren't we the same tribe?

BARRY. Wow! That's interesting.

PATRICK. No it's not.

BARRY. It is. She WANTS to be in their tribe. But what tribe would that be?

NICK. The tribe of people who drink Chardonnay.

MARGO. I don't want to be in their tribe.

BARRY. You just said you did want to be in their tribe.

MARGO. I didn't say I wanted to be in their tribe I said –

PATRICK. You said –

MARGO. Don't tell me what I –

PATRICK. You said not even thirty seconds ago –

MARGO. You're not even listening to what I said you're not allowed to tell me what I said!

PATRICK. Not thirty seconds ago you said –

MARGO. WHAT I SAID WAS – I can't remember what I said.

PATRICK. You do, you hate gay people.

MARGO. I DON'T HATE GAY PEOPLE. I HATE THE SHITHEADS AT WORK.

BARRY. So why don't you get another job?

MARGO. I'm good at what I do, why should I have to get another job? I put fifteen years into that place. Doing – do any of you even know what I do?

(There's a pause.)

LILA. You work in an office.

BARRY. Yeah, that's pretty much, like office stuff?

MARGO. Right? Right? You know why you don't know what I do? Because that's how stupid it is.

BARRY. I'm sure it's interesting.

MARGO. It's not interesting! Why do you think I'm so mad about it? I'm so BORED down there I want to kill myself! I'm so much better than them and I didn't, I sold myself out for fifteen years just because I was – I thought, if I was good, if I was just good – and it's stupid, I can't even talk about it, that's how stupid it is, what I do. The fact that I cared about that job is so pathetic I can't even and the fact that I'm so good at it is even worse! And it was nothing but a lie the whole time. I just thought, god, such stupid pride, that someday they would have to admit, they were taking credit for my work the whole time and I sucked it up because that's what you tell yourself, you can't afford to be, you have to be a team player! And they don't even, they don't see me. They don't even... I'm not seen. And now they know that I see them. They feel me seeing them.

(A breath.)

My youth. I gave up my youth for nothing.

(She puts her head down on her hands. After a moment LILA goes to her.)

LILA. You okay?

MARGO. I'm sorry. Seriously. I'm so grateful for this place. I feel terrible, I never ordered your steak dinner. Of course you need people to do that, how can you make any money if people don't help? Nobody is helping anyone anymore. That's what it feels like. Like we're not the same tribe, none of us, we're not...anything. Or not that we're not anything. Just that we're one thing. And god help you if you don't, if that's not...and I can't even, oh my god.

(Then:)

Am I drunk?

LILA. You might be.

PATRICK. Might be?

(A beat.)

MARGO. Well, it's a bar. So we all might be drunk.

PATRICK. Some might be and some are.

LILA. Oh knock it off.

PATRICK. Now I'm not even allowed to talk? So that's what the rules are now, the men aren't even allowed to voice an opinion now?

NICK. No.

LILA. Yeah, those are the rules.

NICK. Those are not the rules.

PATRICK. Because that's what's wrong with the world. You want to know the truth that's why places like this don't make sense anymore.

MARGO. They do make sense. That's my point, that's what I –

PATRICK. You create these rules. This is how people are supposed to act. They don't act the way I want so they're bad people. They're mean to me at my job so now I'm going to go get drunk and tell everyone down there at the Crow's Nest that gay people are evil.

MARGO. That is not what I said and you know it –

LILA. *(Overlap.)* That's not what she said –

PATRICK. *(Overlap.)* You come in here and you take over and no one else is allowed to talk and that is the world now. People staring at devices, you see the kids on the street staring at these tiny, in their hands, and that's how they talk to each other now. This, what we're doing here, no one is talking. So be it. I grew up in this bar. Nicky and I, we came here in college, this was our bar, this was our neighborhood, my dad used to come here and drink with Lila's dad, Nicky and Lila, they met in this bar. This is our world, this is our history. You showed up, I don't know when you started coming here, I'm not saying you don't belong here, anyone can come here. But you don't get to just decide you know what it is. Because your rules are screwy. This shit you're saying about hating gay people.

MARGO. I don't hate gay people. I hate being alone.

PATRICK. Everybody's alone. Some of us just don't whine about it.

BARRY. Come on, that's not fair. You got to be fair now. We all go through things, you can't say she's not entitled to her feelings.

PATRICK. I didn't say that.

BARRY. You did say that, you're telling her she's not allowed to talk.

PATRICK. I'm saying –

BARRY. Don't tell me what you're saying –

PATRICK. I'm just talking!

BARRY. So is she.

(*To* **MARGO.**) It sounds disappointing, what you're going through. Fifteen years at a job, whether you like it or not, you got to be able to rely on the people you work with. I worked a lot of different jobs over the years and I didn't particularly love any of them, the best part of my day was lunch or you know, a couple of minutes in the break room. Resting my legs on the coffee table. And just jawing a little, with the guys. Blowing off steam. The couple of jobs I worked, I didn't have anybody to talk to? It made for a long day.

MARGO. It does.

BARRY. You know what? I have an idea what might make you feel a little better.

(*He gets up and goes to the jukebox.*)

MARGO. I feel fine.

BARRY. No you don't.

(*He gets out a couple quarters and puts them in the jukebox.*)

PATRICK. You got to be kidding me.

BARRY. I am not kidding.

NICK. That thing doesn't work, Barry.

BARRY. I did this thing. It might work.

NICK. That thing hasn't worked in years.

BARRY. I'm not kidding, there was this thing I did, I'm pretty sure I figured out why it wasn't working.

(*Music up. A song in the style of Sam Cooke plays.** **MARGO** *laughs;* **LILA** *cheers.*)

---

*A license to produce *The Nest* does not include a performance license for any third-party or copyrighted music. Licensees should create an original composition or use music in the public domain. For further information, please see Music Use Note on page 3.

NICK. You got to be kidding me.

BARRY. It was unplugged.

> *(He holds out his arm to* **MARGO**. *She accepts the offer. They dance.* **NICK** *looks at the back of the jukebox.)*

NICK. That can't be what the problem was.

BARRY. Somebody unplugged it.

NICK. Yeah, because it wasn't working.

BARRY. I don't know about that. 'Cause it's working now.

> *(As* **NICK** *and* **PATRICK** *look at the back of the jukebox,* **MARGO** *and* **BARRY** *dance for a moment.)*

NICK. That is –

> *(The music stops.)*

LILA. Oh no.

BARRY. Oh man. What'd you do to it.

NICK. I swear to god, I didn't touch it. I just looked at it.

> *(**BARRY** goes over to look at it.)*

BARRY. The connection's probably just loose. You probably just need to replace it.

LILA. We should do that!

NICK. That thing is a piece of junk.

LILA. Come on, it's nice to have some music around here. That was great.

PATRICK. Stop messing with that, you're going to blow the place up.

BARRY. Leave me alone, I'm good at this.

LILA. What do people want on their salads?

MARGO. I'll have ranch.

BARRY. I'll have ranch too.

LILA. Patrick?

PATRICK. So what, are we all having dinner?

LILA. You ordered the steak, I put in the order, you can't unorder the steak. It's cooking!

PATRICK. That's fine, no that's good. I just, you know, my friend is coming over.

NICK. That's tonight?

PATRICK. I told you.

NICK. You didn't say tonight.

LILA. You have a friend coming?

PATRICK. You didn't tell her?

NICK. I told you I needed a little time.

PATRICK. And I told you there wasn't any!

LILA. What are you talking about?

NICK. He has a friend who's going to look at the bar.

LILA. Why?

NICK. He's interested in buying it.

(*Then, fast:*)

Not it, not selling the bar. We wouldn't sell. Just the bartop and the mirror. They're worth a lot of money.

(*A beat.*)

LILA. Can I speak to you for a minute.

(*She heads for the kitchen.*)

NICK. We can talk out here.

(**LILA** *turns, stunned at this. The others don't know what to do.*)

This isn't a big deal.

(*He pours himself a drink. There is a terrible pause while* **LILA** *realizes he is going to hold his ground, in front of everybody.*)

LILA. I didn't agree to this.

NICK. There's nothing to agree to.

PATRICK. He's just coming over.

LILA. Patrick, do you mind?

PATRICK. Well, I do mind, because this guy is a friend of mine.

NICK. I told you about this.

LILA. You didn't tell me about this!

NICK. I said, I wanted to have a conversation and you agreed.

LILA. I said yes we should talk –

NICK. Well we can't talk about it unless we have the facts.

LILA. I'm sorry, you guys –

BARRY. It's okay.

NICK. It's not that big a deal.

PATRICK. It's not a little deal. This guy is coming from Chicago.

LILA. He's a friend of yours?

PATRICK. Yeah.

LILA. Well, you didn't talk to me about this, Patrick. I don't know why the two of you went behind my back –

NICK. Nobody went behind your back!

PATRICK. He's allowed to ask for the information. You can't tell him –

LILA. Hey.

PATRICK. I'm trying to help here.

LILA. Well, this isn't helping!

NICK. *(Pissed now.)* You don't even want to let someone come in and tell us how much it might be worth to just give us a ballpark figure, if we wanted to sell not the whole place just the bar and the mirror. Just to know what it's worth.

PATRICK. You need to have the information, Lila.

LILA. What I need is a little breathing room.

PATRICK. Yeah but life doesn't always give you what you think you need.

LILA. Patrick, I'm not kidding.

PATRICK. Lila I've known you a long time longer than Nicky even. Your dad was everything to me.

LILA. Nevertheless, Nick and I are trying to have a conversation.

PATRICK. You guys are trying a lot of things here, to keep the place going, everybody knows business isn't what it was. You got to know what your options are. Just to know, if you had to sell, what would you get?

LILA. What kind of a place would we have left if we did that? We'd have no place. People come here because it's beautiful, because there's a sense of time and elegance and and and –

NICK. People come here to get drunk! Or, they don't come here at all!

LILA. People do come here.

NICK. No they don't. They're all going to TGI Fridays.

LILA. Yes, and those places are horrible. At least we still have a little history.

NICK. History but no customers. Come on! Don't you want to be somewhere where where where – life is going on?

LILA. Life is going on here.

NICK. Look around!

(He pours himself a shot, then another.)

Sorry, guys. No offense.

BARRY. None taken.

MARGO. I'm offended.

PATRICK. You're always offended.

NICK. Seriously I apologize. Let me top you off.

(He does.)

MARGO. *(Cautious.)* You guys are selling The Nest?

LILA. No.

NICK. So now we're not even having the conversation? Because I don't know how to have a conversation without facts. This is, agreed, your family legacy, everybody respects that. But twenty-five years of my life are in this place and that means I have equity. This isn't a situation where you get to just be the last word.

(Behind her the door opens; a woman enters.
LILA *turns to greet her.)*

LILA. *(To* **WOMAN**.*)* Hello!

WOMAN. Hi. I'm meeting some friends.

LILA. Oh yes! That's right. They said, they told me they
were spreading the word. Come on in.

WOMAN. Good. Wow. This place is gorgeous. That bar is
gorgeous.

LILA. *(Clipped.)* Thank you.

(Across the room, **MARGO** *leans in to listen to*
PATRICK *and* **NICK**.*)*

MARGO. You guys both suck.

PATRICK. Oh that's great.

MARGO. You totally went behind her back –

NICK. Nobody went behind anyone's back –

MARGO. Yeah but why did he come to you? Why didn't you
tell her?

NICK. I did –

MARGO. You didn't, you were afraid, or you just didn't want
to have a conversation with the girl –

PATRICK. Oh my god.

MARGO. This is just like my work.

NICK. *(Overlap.)* Look, everyone relax. We were just talking
about having someone come appraise the place. It's not
a big deal.

MARGO. She's not the one who made a big deal out of it.
You are.

PATRICK. Actually, you are.

MARGO. Okay I accept that. But why do you want them to
sell this place, anyway? You like spent your whole life
here and it's nice. Why would you want them to sell it?

NICK. We are not selling the bar! We are talking about
selling the bartop... Not the bar. The BAR. We're not
even selling that, we were just – never mind.

LILA. *(To* **WOMAN***.)* I am so sorry. We're just in the middle of something. What can we get you?

WOMAN. I'm actually here to – I'm the person who's coming, to look at the bar. I'm meant to meet –

PATRICK. Me! You're meeting me!

(He stands, excited.)

MARGO. You're meeting, him?

WOMAN. Sam Nachmanoff. Hello.

PATRICK. You're Sam! She's Sam. Sam Nachmanoff.

MARGO. Your "friend."

PATRICK. I didn't say she was my friend.

MARGO. You did, you so did.

NICK. You did, man, just let it go. Hi, how's it going I'm Nick Freelander, this is my place.

LILA. It's our place.

SAM. So great to meet you!

PATRICK. Hi, hi, I'm Patrick Wilcox, I'm Jimmy's friend –

SAM. Jimmy?

PATRICK. In your office, he's the one I talked to about the bar and he said you'd be coming by –

SAM. James?

PATRICK. That's right. James. I talked to James.

MARGO. But he doesn't actually own the bar. He drinks here.

PATRICK. But I was the one who spoke to James about it.

SAM. I'm so glad you did! It's glorious.

LILA. I'm afraid you might be out here on a little bit of a wild goose chase. We actually are not interested in selling at this time.

SAM. Okay.

NICK. But we are interested. In a kind of general way. About what it might be worth. So that we can have a conversation about it. Just know what our options are.

SAM. I can see why; it really is gorgeous. And from the street, you honestly wouldn't know this was in here! Is this hand-carved?

NICK. We think so. We're pretty sure.

LILA. *(Annoyed at this.)* It's actually an heirloom. A family – my great-great – great – grandfather –

NICK. It goes back a good long, eighteen sixty something –

SAM. He carved it himself?

NICK. That's kind of more of a rumor –

LILA. So says the skeptic, but we do have a photograph.

> *(She takes it off the back of the bar, shows it to* SAM.*)*

SAM. *(Pronouncing it properly.)* A daguerreotype.

LILA. That's right.

SAM. And this is –

LILA. My great-great-great-great, I don't know how many greats, honestly –

SAM. It's fantastic –

LILA. He was, they say he was a clockmaker –

SAM. *(Comparing to photo.)* Look! It's identical.

PATRICK. *(Taking over.)* So I don't know what Jimmy told you, but as you can see –

SAM. Mahogany.

PATRICK. That's right, mahogany.

SAM. It's in pristine condition.

PATRICK. Pristine is right.

NICK. The mirror is also original to the period, as you can see from the photograph.

PATRICK. The daurrogotype.

SAM. This is honestly, just gorgeous.

PATRICK. It's all exactly as it was, as you can see.

SAM. This place is a work of art. Honestly, it's thrilling. Just thrilling.

(She reaches over and squeezes **NICK***'s arm, happy.)*

You're doing the right thing, getting it appraised. This is very, very impressive.

*(***IRENE*** and* **NED** *enter.* **NED** *waves, sheepish.)*

NED. Hey.

IRENE. Hey.

LILA. Hey!

BARRY. Hey hey it's the rock 'em sock 'em robots!

NED. *(Laughing.)* Yeah okay.

IRENE. Oh my god we were so mortified we came back last night to apologize, did she tell you?

MARGO. She did.

IRENE. So sorry.

MARGO. Not at all, you were very entertaining.

BARRY. Yeah, we liked it.

NED. Well, we are still mortified. Can we buy you a drink?

MARGO. I'm a single lady who hangs out in bars. Yes, you can buy me a drink.

BARRY. But the fries are on me.

NED. The fries are on ME. At least, they were on me. And it wasn't the first time.

IRENE. Oh don't do that.

NED. Don't do what.

IRENE. Don't, oh my god I'm already totally mortified. It's not like I throw fries at you every night.

NED. Don't you?

IRENE. Don't make jokes! They don't know us!
(To others.) We were very well-behaved last night.

LILA. They absolutely were. Grab a seat. Nick, can you take their drink order?

NICK. Yeah yeah just a sec.

SAM. Can I go back here?

NICK. Sure.

> *(For **SAM** has leaned in and is whispering something to him. Then she laughs, loud. He nods, interested. **LILA** clocks this, a little pissed now, and goes into the kitchen.)*

BARRY. So, you're not a doctor? Excuse me.

NED. Oh me.

> *(He looks around. **BARRY** waves to him.)*

BARRY. Lila said, you're not a doctor.

NED. No, I'm a climatologist. I'm a post-doc up at the university.

MARGO. And you're Irene. Women's studies.

IRENE. You know my name?

BARRY. They told us.

MARGO. Seriously we talked for hours about you.

NED. Surely you have better things to talk about.

MARGO. Sadly, we don't!

BARRY. I was really interested in your point about disease. When you were talking about all those diseases.

IRENE. Oh please don't get him started.

NED. What? He's interested.

BARRY. I was curious about the monkeys.

NED. The monkeys.

IRENE. Don't do this to me again. I mean it.

> *(**LILA** re-enters with salads.)*

LILA. Here we go! Three house salads, with ranch dressing.

IRENE. Do not get him started on the monkeys.

BARRY. See I knew there was something about those monkeys.

MARGO. What monkeys?

BARRY. When he was talking about diseases! He mentioned the monkeys.

> *(**LILA** slides by **NICK** and **SAM**.)*

LILA. *(Edgy.)* Nick, where are you at with those drink orders?

SAM. My fault, my fault, I've been monopolizing him.

LILA. Well. Stop that.

(**NICK** *hops to, to get drinks to people.*)

NICK. What can I get you?

IRENE. A martini. I'm going to need one, if he's going to start talking about those monkeys –

NED. The monkeys were in this lab, outside Washington.

BARRY. That's right! Monkeys in Washington, that's what he said!

NED. Let me explain the epidemiology.

IRENE. Here we go. Two martinis.

SAM. You know what? That looks delicious. Could I have one of them?

LILA. Oh you want food.

SAM. That looks so good. No dressing, just a slice of lemon would be great.

(**LILA** *goes.*)

NED. We do have to back it up a little, because people don't know this part. Monkeys plus bat guano equals the ebola virus.

BARRY. I knew that's what it was about.

IRENE. Ned, just understand, these are nice people in a bar –

NED. People are interested in this. I'll make it fast. As we all know, the ebola virus came from Africa. What you might not know is what it does to you, I mean, what it does to the human body, is catastrophic. It melts your internal organs. Like, your insides melt, and then you're puking and shitting blood and your eyes bleed and your ears too I think, I'm not sure, but just, your internal organs are like, if you can imagine a wet bedsheet being ripped in half. That's what it sounds like when your insides burst. And then you're just spewing out of every place you possibly can, you're just...

BARRY. Wooooow.

NED. Yes.

MARGO. That's disgusting.

IRENE. I told you.

NED. It's worse than disgusting. It's also highly contagious. Because the virus wants community. It wants the next person. So everybody gets it and no one survives. Like in Africa, we haven't heard the whole story, trust me. About the horror show that was. And yeah, they contained those few cases, when it showed up in America, but trust me, they threw everything at that. Like, they basically surrounded those people with eight layers of human-sized condoms, so yeah, they contained it. But you have to do that, you really have to – or the human race is done for.

IRENE. Ned! We have to order. Here.

SAM. I've never seen marble work this delicate is so so rare.

*(She hands the menu to **NED**.)*

MARGO. So who do you work for?

SAM. Excuse me?

MARGO. Lila said she's not selling, so there's not likely to be a sale, so is this really worth your time?

SAM. Well, I'm here.

PATRICK. No one said there wouldn't be a sale.

MARGO. Lila said it. I heard her loud and clear.

PATRICK. This is a first step. Information gathering.

MARGO. What was your name? Sam?

SAM. Nachmanoff.

MARGO. I mean, what's your job title?

SAM. My field of expertise is historical architecture.

MARGO. They pay people for that? 'Cause that totally just sounds like something you'd major in in college, but no one will ever give you a job.

SAM. It's a real job. If someone like Nick wanted to hire me I would evaluate his property, break down the numbers and then if it made sense he could decide if he wants me to broker a sale.

MARGO. Lila, you mean.

NICK. We own the bar together.

(**IRENE** *approaches, catching the end of this.*)

IRENE. You're selling the bar?

PATRICK. Just the stuff. Not the bar. So your plan would be to break up everything that's in here –

SAM. I don't have a plan.

PATRICK. But that would be one way to do it, theoretically.

SAM. The smart thing might be to take both pieces. Or, you might want to sell just one element. For instance, the mirror is in superb condition, and the size is impressive. The bevel is deep, and the carving – most pieces from the period are plaster or gesso on wood. This is solid wood gilded with twenty-four-carat gold leaf. This might well be sixteenth century, Venetian, they're absurdly rare.

NICK. Venetian? Come on.

SAM. Who knows. Your great-great-clockmaker may have brought it with him. If he was a craftsman –

NICK. We don't know what he was –

PATRICK. How much is it worth?

SAM. It's worth what someone will pay for it. It would easily take twenty thousand at an auction house, but if you went to private buyers, the right people, you could be looking at more.

PATRICK. How much more?

SAM. Well, determining that would be a process. Just off the top of my head, I would not recommend breaking these up. The curve of the bartop echoes the carvings on the upper corners of the mirror.

It would be valuable in and of itself, this is Crema Valencia marble inlaid with Nembro Rosato and Rosa Peralba. Is it possible this was imported as well?

NICK. (*Excited and bewildered.*) I don't know. We really, we don't know much.

SAM. The rosewood inlay is exquisite.

PATRICK. I told Jim, it was special. This place is really special, you know. No question. This place is special.

NICK. *(More and more intrigued.)* So you would want to take the whole place? Like, the whole room? Because the rest of the furniture isn't really part of it.

SAM. The lighting fixtures are period.

NICK. The lighting fixtures? I don't know how long those have been here. Maybe from the beginning, I don't know.

SAM. There are a lot of museums out there –

PATRICK. A museum!

MARGO. You mean like as one of those rooms, that people stand behind the rope and look in?

NICK. How much would a museum pay for something like this, the bar and the mirror, and the –

SAM. I'd have to do some more research. Honestly, this place is a gem. You'd need to handle it carefully. But it could bring in two-fifty, three hundred?

NICK. Thousand?

SAM. Hire me, and I'll find out.

NICK. *(Excited.)* You're hired, baby, you're hired!

> *(He hugs her, picks her up, and swings her around.)*

SAM. Oh my goodness!

> *(LILA enters, carrying two plates.)*

LILA. Here we go, steak frites for...

> *(She sees SAM in NICK's arms. SAM is laughing, giddy. It's a little awkward.)*

Everything okay, honey?

> *(NICK follows her as she delivers the food.)*

NICK. Yeah, we've been talking about you know, what it might look like to just sell off part of the bar. I know you have reservations, but she says there's a lot, we could really make a good amount of money out of this.

LILA. You know, I have to – I have two more steak dinners in there, I could really use a hand.

NED. And chicken wings and fries and a house salad.

IRENE. Two house salads.

NED. I'm not going to have one.

IRENE. You haven't eaten anything green for three days. Two house salads.

(LILA goes. NICK takes a moment, then turns to SAM.)

NICK. So what do we need to do to get this process going?

SAM. Let me get out some contracts, you should have them in hand when you discuss this.

PATRICK. You should trust her, Nick. She comes highly recommended. Jimmy says she's like a shark.

SAM. *(Laughing.)* That's flattering.

PATRICK. No no, that's what we want, we want a shark. A shark for our side. Jimmy is totally reliable.

(LILA enters with two more dinners.)

LILA. Okay both of these are a little bloody, but that's what they recommend.

(She sets them down for PATRICK and NICK.)

SAM. You know what? That looks terrific.

LILA. Did you want to order one?

NICK. It's on us.

PATRICK. Here, you have mine and I'll wait. It's fine, I'll wait. Here, you want my salad?

SAM. I'm supposed to be getting my own.

(She looks at LILA, smiles, apologetic.)

PATRICK. Take mine, take mine.

LILA. She doesn't want dressing. Just a little lemon. Sorry, I'm by myself back there.

SAM. Not a problem.

(LILA disappears into the kitchen again.)

IRENE. *(To* NICK.*)* Are you really selling this place? Because I just think that would be a huge mistake.

PATRICK. Whoa whoa whoa –

MARGO. Don't tell her whoa –

PATRICK. You don't get a vote!

MARGO. If we don't get a vote why do you get a vote?

PATRICK. You know what? You're hostile.

MARGO. I'm what?

PATRICK. You are you're –

MARGO. I'm asking a question –

PATRICK. You're not asking a question. You're interfering in something you don't know anything about.

MARGO. Interfering?

PATRICK. *(To* SAM.*)* So, you know a lot about this stuff. Rosa perabla, neblata cremada –

SAM. Oh god! I know. I'm such a nerd.

> *(She laughs at herself a little.)*

ALL GUYS. *(Reassuring.)* No no, oh no, no no no.

NICK. I wouldn't say that you're a nerd. Hardly.

SAM. Well, you're very kind. I'm always afraid I may be overcompensating a little. I have to travel a lot, just coming in and out of places all the time, it can be a little intimidating.

PATRICK. We are not about that at all.

SAM. Thank you. I can see that.

NED. So your job is like running around the country and evaluating?

SAM. Evaluating. That's exactly the right word.

MARGO. So you go to different cities and look around, for targets –

SAM. No no no, I was invited –

NICK. She was invited.

PATRICK. She was totally invited.

SAM. And I offer whatever I can.

MARGO. But this is on spec, your opinion, about what this place might be worth, it's –

SAM. Absolutely.

MARGO. It's just, you're giving away a lot of information –

SAM. I'm not giving anything away. If people feel that I'm the right person to broker a deal, I will be well compensated. I do occasionally get a little overly enthusiastic but that comes from passion more than anything.

NED. That's clear.

SAM. Oh god, my brothers used to make fun of me all the time. They always thought I was showing off.

NED. No!

SAM. I really do just love this stuff. It's so beautiful. It's a privilege just to touch it. And if I can help find a place for it, where more people can appreciate and enjoy it – it's just a great job.

PATRICK. That's great. So you're doing a service for everybody.

> (**LILA** *re-enters with two green salads which she delivers to* **NED** *and* **IRENE**.)

BARRY. You had a lot of brothers?

SAM. Four. Oh my god. Honestly, it was a little bit like being raised by wolves.

NICK. The wolves did a terrific job.

> (**LILA** *rolls her eyes and exits again.*)

SAM. Thanks.

> (*There is an uncomfortable pause.*)

BARRY. This is delicious. Seriously, when she gave us those steaks last night and they were like blocks of ice, I thought I don't know how this is supposed to work. And you know then my son called and I told him, you know, I have this frozen steak, someone gave me a frozen steak, at this bar I go to sometimes but this can't be any good right? And he was like, where have you been, Dad? They send steak through the mail all the time now. He gets them from clients, which he's not supposed to accept, but what are you going to do, they show up at your doorstep, you can't actually send them back, you have to put them in the freezer and then you'd be crazy not to eat them. Anyway he has experience with frozen steaks, and he said you know, it's delicious, it's the best steak in the country, they know how to freeze it, just taste it. And he's right. These things are incredible.

SAM. They really are!

(She is eating.)

NICK. *(To SAM.)* Is that too red for you?

SAM. Are you kidding? I live on raw meat.

(She laughs, flirtatious.)

PATRICK. Now that's what I'm talking about!

MARGO. You know, Nicky, I could use a refill.

NICK. Sure sure sure. How about you, Barry, you okay?

BARRY. I wouldn't say no.

NICK. Sam?

SAM. Do you have a good shiraz, or a, just something that's not too heavy? Not as light as a pinot, just not a bordeaux, or a cab.

NICK. Sure.

PATRICK. Nothing too heavy, Nick.

(He sits with SAM.)

So. When I talked to Jim, he said you were the best in the business, and that if we really had something here, you would be the person who would know.

SAM. That's nice.

PATRICK. It's not nice; I'm just telling you what he said. So I'm not someone to dance around the mulberry bush. Can I presume that you're aware of our arrangement?

SAM. "Arrangement"?

PATRICK. Of the discussions, where my part comes in, you're aware of that, right? He didn't talk to you? I'm the one, this whole thing is my idea. So he told me, I should be talking to you about my participation. Well Jimmy indicated that it would be a percentage situation.

SAM. Did he?

PATRICK. He indicated this to you, right?

SAM. I actually don't know Jimmy all that well.

PATRICK. The point is, he made the arrangement, on my recommendation, for you to come out here.

MARGO. What was the arrangement?

PATRICK. The arrangement was –

MARGO. 'Cause see –

> *(This picks up steam.)*

PATRICK. The arrangement –

MARGO. That actually is all I –

PATRICK. The arrangement –

BARRY. No no no –

MARGO. No what?

> *(The conversations start to tumble on top of each other.)*

BARRY. It's not what you –

PATRICK. Was not, was not –

BARRY. It was just this guy –

PATRICK. She is –

MARGO. I am what, hostile?

BARRY. *(Overlap.)* They knew each other from –

SAM. Like I said it was just a referral –

BARRY. *(Overlap.)* A pick-up basketball game, or softball, and he knew this other guy, Jimmy.

SAM. And I said I would –

PATRICK. Yeah and he said there would be a percentage involved.

SAM. I don't know anything –

BARRY. *(Overlap.)* So he doesn't know this Jimmy guy but he definitely knows the first guy.

SAM. I generally don't talk numbers until I've had more time to make a specific recommendation.

NICK. That makes sense. Why don't you take a little more time to put together your thoughts and then we can see what we're looking at. And then we can take it from there.

SAM. That sounds terrific.

(**NICK** *brings her a glass of wine.*)

IRENE. Well, I don't care how much she says they'll pay you for it. Bars don't belong in museums. That's the dumbest idea I ever heard. If people think it's such a great idea to get a good look at a historic piece of architecture, why don't they just come out here and have a drink? You can enjoy all the architecture you want and also get a nice buzz, not to mention a steak dinner.

NED. If you had a vote, you mean.

IRENE. Everyone's voting. Isn't everyone voting?

NED. (*To others.*) Sorry.

IRENE. Don't apologize for me.

NED. That's not what I'm doing, I'm just trying to make it –

IRENE. (*Overlap.*) It's exactly what you're doing, Ned –

PATRICK. Hey. Why don't you two take it outside.

(*To* **SAM.**) How are those numbers adding up?

IRENE. Whoa. Did he just tell us to leave?

NED. It's fine. Don't –

IRENE. "Don't"?

NED. Oh boy.

(**SAM** *smiles at* **PATRICK,** *polite.*)

SAM. I'm sorry, Patrick, but you're not actually a legal party to this.

PATRICK. I'm not a legal party now?

SAM. My understanding is that Nick owns the bar.

MARGO. Lila owns the bar.

NICK. We're married; we own it together.

SAM. That's right. Nick, anytime you're ready.

*(She gives **NICK** some documents. **NICK** looks at **PATRICK**.)*

PATRICK. Sure sure. I totally get it. I got it.

(He goes to the bar, sits there.)

What's a guy got to do to get a drink around here?

*(This clips **LILA**, who is re-entering with the chicken fingers and fries.)*

LILA. Well, give me a minute, Patrick, I was just trying to stay on top of the food orders.

*(She sees **NICK** and **SAM** going over papers. **SAM** puts her arm on **NICK**'s shoulder and smiles at him, leans in to explain something.)*

*(To **SAM**.)* Everything okay over there?

SAM. Absolutely, Nick and I are just getting a handle on what needs to happen.

*(She smiles at **NICK** again. **LILA** delivers the food and comes over.)*

LILA. And what's that?

NICK. We can talk about it later.

LILA. I don't want to talk about it later.

NICK. Lila, I got this. I'm collecting information. I told you I was going to do that, and we can talk about it later. We don't need you.

*(**LILA** reacts, stuck.)*

NED. *(Oblivious.)* Can we get another order of fries?

*(After a heartbeat, **LILA** heads for the kitchen, steely.)*

IRENE. Oh boy.

NED. Oh boy what.

IRENE. *(Covering for all of them.)* Oh boy that's just the way, isn't it? The historic places are just evaporating.

NICK. *(Sharp.)* Nothing's evaporating.

PATRICK. Oh, I disagree. Things are evaporating. Every day, something that we value, something that meant something, it just fades away. Honor. Trust. Decency. Friendship, loyalty to your friends. All the things that a place like this symbolizes, it just means less and less in the world, and then we're left with nothing.

MARGO. Whoa whoa whoa, what?

NED. That's what I mean! The human race has a tragic flaw.

IRENE. A what?

NED. A tragic flaw! As a race we are blinded by the little picture. Greed.

PATRICK. That's right, greed –

NED. Self-interest –

PATRICK. Self-interest!

NED. We are all going to be, you know, murdered by microbes! And we could stop it, the science is in place to stop it! But will we? That's what I mean.

IRENE. Oh my god. You don't mean anything. He doesn't mean anything.

NED. What are you –

IRENE. You don't mean anything. You're just looking for an excuse to get back to those monkeys so you can just head down that road again.

NED. Okay "road"? This is an argument. This is the truth!

IRENE. *(To others.)* The truth! Oh, please. This is what he does.

NED. I don't "do" anything. You're the one who does that that woman thing –

IRENE. What "woman" thing?

NED. Aw, come on.

IRENE. I'm serious. What thing?

NED. The "I'm a women's studies professor so everything is about gender all the time even when we're eating breakfast. Or lunch. Or dinner." We can be talking about anything, anything at all, would you like ketchup with your fries, and the next thing you know, it's all men do this, and men do that and a woman would never do that –

IRENE. That's hilarious.

NED. Here we go.

NICK. Guys –

IRENE. Everywhere you look on planet Earth men own the means of communication, the movies are all about men, television shows –

MARGO. CORPORATIONS –

IRENE. And in case anyone's forgotten corporations as it turns out are people who are allowed to throw as much money around as they want because speech is FREE ha ha except for women.

NICK. Guys –

NED. This is what you do.

IRENE. Genocide. War. Poisoning the earth.

MARGO. Rape. Murder.

IRENE. Football games.

MARGO. Hooters.

IRENE. Guns. Carnage. And what do we do? We TALK too much?

BARRY. Just don't throw the fries.

SAM. You have a very lively place here.

NICK. Yeah. Look guys –

PATRICK. I agree with him, though. I do.

IRENE. Don't agree with him.

PATRICK. Nothing means anything to anyone. People betray you without thinking twice. And it means nothing.

MARGO. What are you talking about?

PATRICK. I'm talking –

MARGO. You are unbelievable –

PATRICK. I'm just –

MARGO. Betray, what planet are you –

PATRICK. I'm making an obser–

MARGO. You brought this person in, this totally other person and you started this whole chain of events around things that aren't even your business!

PATRICK. An observation and I was not –

MARGO. This isn't your PROPERTY. You're trying to act like –

PATRICK. I was doing a favor for a friend –

MARGO. You're not doing a favor for anyone! This isn't a favor for Lila!

NICK. Hey hey hey –

MARGO. This isn't a favor for me!

PATRICK. I never said I was doing a favor for you –

NICK. Nobody is doing anything –

PATRICK. That's a lie.

NICK. That's a what?

MARGO. This is a con–

NICK. Whoa whoa –

SAM. This is maybe not a great time –

PATRICK. *(Off* MARGO.*)* Look she's not anybody –

MARGO. Neither are you!

SAM. *(To* NICK.*)* I will call you –

NICK. Thanks –

BARRY. You don't know the whole picture here –

MARGO. Oh god no shit –

PATRICK. Don't talk to her –

MARGO. Don't TALK to me? I don't even –

PATRICK. This has nothing to do with you!

MARGO. Who are you to tell ANYONE not to talk to me?

> (LILA *re-enters with the last set of fries just as this starts to heat up. She listens, arrested, in the door, then steps forward. She forgets the fries as she hears what is going on.)*

BARRY. Okay no no no no no. No. No! Here's the thing. His ex-wife has been making his life hell.

PATRICK. Don't bring that –

BARRY. I mean seriously –

PATRICK. That has nothing –

BARRY. He doesn't talk about it –

PATRICK. Because it's nobody's business –

BARRY. But it's not that he doesn't want to work, or won't work, she's, that's, everyone knows this is a terrible time, there's nothing out there, and she's taking this position, if he doesn't come up with something, in terms of financial contributions to the family situation, he's not allowed to see his kids. I mean this has been going on. So this is obviously, there's other things going on here.

(Silence. LILA steps forward, saddened by this.)

LILA. Patrick, is this true?

PATRICK. It's not that bad.

LILA. How long has this been going on?

PATRICK. A while.

BARRY. Five months. He hasn't seen his kids in five months.

LILA. Oh, Patrick. I'm so sorry.

NED. That's awful.

IRENE. Honey.

NED. You don't think that's awful?

IRENE. I don't know the situation.

NED. How much of the situation do you have to know?

IRENE. That's right –

MARGO. Yeah it really is awful, five months without seeing your kids, horrible. So how long's it been since you paid any child support?

IRENE. Yeah, see that's what I was kind of –

BARRY. Awwww come on.

MARGO. No we're all supposed to feel sorry for him –

PATRICK. No one is feeling sorry for me –

MARGO. Poor Patrick his horrible wife won't let him see his kids –

BARRY. I was just trying to put things in –

MARGO. Who he doesn't support!

PATRICK. That is not –

BARRY. Seriously she's been –

MARGO. She's been what? Asking for MONEY –

BARRY. Asking for a lot of money!

MARGO. For their KIDS?

NICK. Hey hey guys seriously –

PATRICK. None of this –

MARGO. This is classic, you can't support your own family, so you cook up some way to make it someone else's problem.

PATRICK. I never said –

MARGO. He's playing you, Nick!

NICK. Okay okay –

PATRICK. I did it for Nick, he wants out of here –

NICK. We're just talking!

MARGO. So selling his wife's bar is just something you'd do for a bro.

NICK. It's my bar too.

MARGO. That's what buddies do for each other. Help the dude sell his wife's bar. Get him away from her. Give him a new lease on life!

PATRICK. God, I am tired of –

MARGO. And you get to listen to him talk about how his marriage is not what it should be and it hasn't been for a long time –

NICK. Hey –

MARGO. And yours had been on the skids too –

PATRICK. This isn't about that –

MARGO. Not because you're a failure –

BARRY. Whoa –

MARGO. Not because you lost control of your life.

> (**PATRICK** *looks at his scotch glass in his hands.*)

BARRY. Wait –

MARGO. Not becasue you're not fit to even speak to your own kids because you're such a fucking drunk –

> (**PATRICK** *throws his glass at her. She ducks. It hits the mirror. Everyone shouts. The lights shift as the mirror shatters.*)

> (*Everyone looks on in horror.*)

> (*Lights shift again. Silence.* **LILA** *takes a step forward.*)

> (**PATRICK** *takes a step back.*)

LILA. Oh.

MARGO. Oh Lila.

LILA. Oh.

NICK. No. No no no.

PATRICK. I'm sorry. Nick. I –

NICK. Don't talk to me.

MARGO. What did you do.

PATRICK. What did I do? You were the one.

MARGO. Don't you put this on me –

PATRICK. I don't have to put it on you. This is all on you. You've been at everyone all night –

MARGO. I didn't –

PATRICK. Are you going to deny it!

MARGO. I was having a conversation in a bar that doesn't give you the right to physically attack me –

PATRICK. *(Overlap.)* You weren't just having a conversation. You were tearing this place apart.

BARRY. Man, you got to stop this. Back down, man –

MARGO. *(Overlap.)* This is on you, it's all on you –

LILA. Shut up! Everybody SHUT UP.

> *(There is a significant pause.)*

PATRICK. I'll pay for it. Obviously I'll… I'll find the money.

LILA. It's not replaceable.

SAM. That's not necessarily true. Excuse me. Do you mind?

> *(She gestures to the bar, doesn't wait for permission, goes behind and starts to look at the broken mirror.)*

The frame isn't damaged, that's where the concern would be. But it looks…

> *(She stops for a moment, then feels what may be a crack.)*

NICK. What. WHAT.

SAM. It's a shame, no question. Sixteenth-century Venetian glass, there's just not that much of it out there. But it really wouldn't affect the bigger picture. I know of four buyers off the top of my head, who would still be interested. The glass, you just replace it. If you popped in something from the nineteenth century most people won't even notice.

PATRICK. Wait a minute. It's okay?

NICK. It's not okay.

PATRICK. Not okay, I don't mean that. But you could still…

SAM. Sell it? You can sell anything.

PATRICK. Wow.

> *(Then:)*

Wow.

LILA. How much was it worth?

SAM. It's impossible to put a number on situations. I don't know specifically, obviously, who the buyer would be. It all depends. So I'm not sure what you're asking.

LILA. I'm asking how much – how much – it's broken now, he broke it –

PATRICK. I didn't –

LILA. How much was it worth?

SAM. The glass itself, if it was what I think – maybe ten, twenty thousand.

LILA. Ten or twenty?

SAM. Yes.

LILA. No, that's a real question. Which is it, ten or twenty. There's a big difference.

SAM. Not really, since it's worth nothing now.

LILA. Okay. Yes, I see that, yes, but isn't it your job, I mean, that's what your job would be, if we hired you, to sell this place, your job would be to tell us how much we could expect to get for all of, for for for everything, and you can't even tell the difference between ten and twenty THOUSAND. If you can't tell me what a broken mirror used to be worth, why would I trust you to sell –

(She stops herself. She is really mad.)

SAM. Yes, I see your point.

(Then, to **NICK***.)* Well, the numbers are there, and you have my card. So if you want to talk further, or move ahead with this in any way, you know how to get in touch with me.

(She smiles and turns to go.)

LILA. What do you mean, "move ahead with this in any way"? What is THAT supposed to mean?

SAM. It just means that if either of you have questions about selling your beautiful property, you can call me.

LILA. Yeah but you didn't talk to me about it. You talked to him. Why did you do that?

SAM. I'm talking to both of you.

LILA. Everybody told you. It's my bar. It's, my great-great – grandfather. He was a clockmaker.

(She stops herself. **NICK** *nods.)*

NICK. We'll give you a call.

SAM. I'd like that.

> *(She exits. There is a moment of silence.)*

IRENE. I don't know about anyone else. But I could use a
drink.

LILA. Help yourself.

IRENE. Seriously?

LILA. I'm not about to wait on anybody right now.

MARGO. I'll do it.

> *(She goes behind the bar.* **BARRY** *joins her.*
> *They start to serve drinks.)*

LILA. "I'd like that." "I'd like that." Oooo I'd love to talk to
you about your "property."

IRENE. She was kind of creepy.

NICK. She was fine.

MARGO. Oh please. That dress.

IRENE. Seriously. That was not the dress of someone who
wants to buy your "property."

NICK. Well, I hope it's the dress of someone who wants to
sell my property.

MARGO. She tell you all about her love life, in there? How
she loves her work but it's lonely being a woman in a
man's world?

NICK. We were talking business.

MARGO. Sure.

IRENE. I'd get a look at the card.

NED. Irene.

IRENE. I'm serious, I want to see the card.

LILA. I want to see the card too.

NICK. You want to see her card?

LILA. Is that a problem?

NICK. No. That's no, no it's –

> *(He picks up the file of papers and hands the
> whole thing to* **LILA.** *She takes it to the bartop.)*

Look. The good news is, this place is worth something. It's worth a lot. That's the takeaway. She was tossing around significant figures. And now you see how fragile – how easy it is to lose – something – I think we should do it.

IRENE. She gave you her room number. Her hotel and her room number. On the back of the card. Yeah, that's professional.

(A beat.)

NICK. She's going to be in town for a couple more days.

LILA. Isn't that LUCKY.

NICK. Oh for the love of god.

LILA. She was flirting with you. It wasn't just business. She was flirting with you.

MARGO. She totally was. And she was pretty obvious about it.

IRENE. Right? I was embarrassed for her.

NED. I wasn't.

IRENE. Then I'm embarrassed for you, that you thought that was good flirting.

NED. Maybe you should try it sometime.

IRENE. Whoa, what?

NED. When was the last time you flirted with me?

IRENE. When you started talking about ebola all the time!

NICK. She can flirt with me all she wants, as long as she sells my bar for a lot of money.

LILA. It's my bar.

MARGO. It's my bar. I've been coming here for a year. More! It's my bar. And I don't see why you should be allowed to sell it.

PATRICK. Maybe because they own it.

MARGO. A piece of paper.

PATRICK. It's more than you have.

MARGO. You're lost... You're lost, you're lost.

PATRICK. You don't have a say! You don't have equity! You don't have anything!

MARGO. I'm well aware.

> *(She heads for the door, looks back at them, and leaves.)*

PATRICK. Did she pay her tab?

NICK. Forget it.

PATRICK. Seriously. She just walks off like that, and doesn't even, after what she did?

BARRY. Let it go.

PATRICK. I'm serious.

BARRY. So am I.

NED. Let's go.

> *(**IRENE** nods, stands.)*

PATRICK. And these two. They're not exactly innocents either.

IRENE. *(To **LILA**.)* I'm sorry about what happened to your mirror.

PATRICK. Sure, now you're all concerned. You're the whole reason this happened.

IRENE. This place is lovely. I hope it all works out for you.

LILA. Thank you.

PATRICK. What is that supposed to mean?

> *(**IRENE** and **NED** leave.)*

You hope this all "works out"? What does THAT mean? That's classic. They come in here, they make a mess of everything, and then they hope it works out? Well, fuck that. You don't show up and throw a bomb into everything and then just say, "Hope that works out for you!" What fucking bullshit. Life is not quite that simple my friends. Or idiotic. Some people see things a little more deeply. Some people understand the cost.

And what it means to stand up to that, over time. Time. Some of us see time. We see it. Because we live it. And

we know meaning. And that cannot be taken away
from any of us.

BARRY. Come on, man.

PATRICK. Am I wrong? Tell me to my face, I don't know
what I'm talking about. You can't do it.

BARRY. I'm just tired.

PATRICK. You're tired, because I'm right.

> (*He downs his drink. He is weaving, on his
> feet.*)

We did a good thing tonight. We saved The Nest.

BARRY. Yeah, okay.

PATRICK. It was going down. What I did? I did it to save all
of it. Nobody would have anything, if I didn't.

BARRY. Yeah, that's cool.

PATRICK. I saved it.

> (*He heads out the door.* **BARRY** *looks back at*
> **NICK**.)

BARRY. I'm gonna drive him home.

NICK. That's probably a good idea.

> (**BARRY** *follows* **PATRICK** *out the door. There is a
> moment of silence.* **LILA** *heads for the bartop.*)

LILA. Okay you want to talk, let's talk. Did you ask him or
did he ask you?

NICK. I don't –

LILA. Answer the question. Whose idea was this? First. Did
Patrick come to you with this, or did you go to him?

NICK. I went to him.

LILA. When.

NICK. A while ago. It was a while ago. A year ago maybe.

LILA. Fuck you.

NICK. Oh that's great.

LILA. You have been thinking about this for a year?

NICK. Yeah –

LILA. And you never thought to mention it?

NICK. I did mention it and you didn't listen. Every time I said anything at all, all I got back was, "My family," "My great-grandfather," "My this."

LILA. That is not true.

NICK. *(Snapping.)* I am sick of hearing about your family and this bar, my life is in this bar and I am more than this fucking bar! And I do not apologize for wanting a bigger life. I feel like a blank. Every fucking morning. I wake up and I feel nothing. I'm still alive. I can't have nothing.

　　　(A beat.)

LILA. This is our home –

NICK. It's not our home, it's a bar!

LILA. It is –

NICK. It's a bar where people come and get drunk and talk about how the world is ending –

LILA. The world is not –

NICK. The world IS ending, if the microbes in the air don't kill us, we'll kill ourselves or the planet will kill us –

LILA. That is not what –

NICK. And they can still come and get drunk here no one is saying they can't but if I need to RIP THE WALLS out to find SOMETHING then I'm going to do that.

LILA. They're my walls.

NICK. They're not your walls. They're just walls.

LILA. This is so this is so TYPICAL.

NICK. Typical.

LILA. Typical male midlife crisis –

NICK. Don't do that –

LILA. Don't kid yourself –

NICK. I'm not –

LILA. This is panic.

NICK. Panic.

LILA. Dressed up, panic dressed up as some stupid dream.

NICK. Oh that's great –

LILA. You're like a a cowboy all of a sudden, a big old guy on a HORSE who has to to –

NICK. I would actually like to be a cowboy –

LILA. To ride around the plains and shoot people. While your little woman stays back in the town, teaching the children and washing dishes and and cooking and being a servant.

NICK. WE DON'T HAVE CHILDREN. We don't have children, remember? We don't have children.

> *(Silence.)*

LILA. Look. We could – we could…

NICK. It's too late for that.

LILA. There were things we didn't try.

NICK. I'm not talking about that.

LILA. Nick.

NICK. That was then. And it turned out to be nothing. I've already dealt with that. I don't want the rest of everything to turn into nothing.

> *(He pours himself a shot, then another.* **LILA** *watches him toss them back. She sits, thinking about this.)*

And maybe if we had that, this wouldn't have come up. But we don't and so it did. It's like twenty-five years ago I walked in here and then I never left. It's like nothing in here.

LILA. It's not nothing.

NICK. Well I need MORE. What is wrong with saying, asking for MORE –

LILA. More is stupid –

NICK. More is everywhere, Lila! More is big.

LILA. And big is what you want. Big and stupid.

NICK. You're stupid.

LILA. You're stupid!

NICK. I don't apologize for wanting more. I feel it so deeply. There is more in me!

LILA. There is more in all of us!

NICK. I don't care about all of us! I care about me. And I don't apologize for that.

>   *(A beat.)*

LILA. I don't want you to apologize, for anything. I know there's more in you. There is, a universe in you.

NICK. Yes.

LILA. That's why people like bartenders.

>   *(**NICK** shoots her a look.)*

No I mean it. There's something romantic about you guys. That wild spirit, stuck behind a bar. It's our way. Of touching that. I don't know. I just feel something else.

>   *(She sighs and looks around the bar.)*

Like, I know there's a universe that spreads out around us, but it's not, it's not... Like, I know if you went all the way to the edge of space, you'd get to see all those stars. But there wouldn't be people there. There wouldn't be things that had happened. There wouldn't be memory. I feel so much here. It's such a privilege for me, to stand in time. To know that people came here and lived here and did the same things we were doing. I like place. Even a little place. It feels huge to me. It feels like enough.

NICK. *(Unconvinced.)* Enough.

LILA. This is enough for me. If the world did end, I wouldn't care, as long as you were there. And if you died, I would only want to stay in that place, where you were. Because maybe your ghost would be there. If we stay in the place where we lived, then we would get to be together when we died.

>   *(**NICK** has nothing to say to that one.)*

I know it's not, it's not –

NICK. No. It's not. I'm not a ghost.

LILA. Don't kid yourself. We're all ghosts.

> *(A pause. They look at each other, a great distance between them.* **NICK** *is at the door.* **LILA** *behind the bar.)*

Come on. Let me get you a drink. Is there anything I can get you? What can I get you?

> *(He is at the door. She is at the bar.)*
>
> *(Blackout.)*

End of Play